Deal with the Devil

and Other Stories

Deal with the Devil and Other Stories

Maxine O'Callaghan

Five Star
Unity, Maine

Five Star First Edition Mystery Series.
Published in 2001 in conjunction with
Tekno Books and Ed Gorman.

Cover design by Carol Pringle.

Set in 11 pt. Plantin by Minnie B. Raven.

Printed in the United States on permanent paper.

Library of Congress Cataloging-in-Publication Data

O'Callaghan, Maxine.
　　Deal with the Devil and other stories /
　by Maxine O'Callaghan.
　　　　p.　cm.　(Five Star first edition mystery series)
　　　ISBN 0-7862-3142-4 (hc : alk. paper)
　　　1. Detective and mystery stories, American.　I. Title.
　II. Series.
　PS3565.C35 D43　2001
　813′.54—dc21　　　　　　　　　　　　　2001018147

Table of Contents

Introduction 7

Delilah West stories:

A Change of Clients 9

Bad News 24

Deal with the Devil 48

Diamonds Are for Never 51

Somewhere South of Melrose 71

Emma Hartley stories:

The Sweet Old Lady Who Sits in the Park 89

It Takes One to Kill One 96

Other stories:

Sorry, Frank 110

An Insignificant Crime 116

Exit 119

Wolf Winter 123

Is You Is or Is You Ain't Miranda? 135

Survival Instinct 138

Black Is the Color of My True Love's Heart 147

Introduction

Like many writers I started in the short story form. Unlike many writers I got lucky and the first short story I mailed off sold—to *Alfred Hitchcock's Mystery Magazine*. The second—also published in *AHMM* in 1974—profoundly changed my career.

That story, "A Change of Clients," was about a private detective, a female PI named Delilah West. I knew a few things about her: She worked in Orange County, California, she was a widow still mourning her husband, and she had plenty of smarts and attitude. I knew I wanted to write more about her, and I did—six novels to date—a seventh in progress.

Once I started writing those books and the ones I published in a couple other genres, my ideas all seemed to be novel-length, so I produced no short stories for about ten years. Then I was asked to contribute a story to *Murder California Style*, an anthology from the Southern California Chapter of Mystery Writers of America. More requests followed—from *After Hours*, a small-press horror magazine, from Marilyn Wallace who was editing *Sisters in Crime* anthologies, from Bob Randisi for *Lethal Ladies II* and an audio anthology, from my good friend Jill Morgan who has so far coaxed three contributions from me for various anthologies, plus a fourth soon to be written. So, because I find it hard to say no to my friends, my short stories have once again become an important part of my writing career.

Because I've done such a variety of stories, I decided not to give you all of them in chronological order. Instead I've grouped those featuring Delilah West, placed two back to back that star a sweet but deadly old lady named Emma Hartley, and then put the rest in order of publication rather than try to do any more sorting. The last two are new, published here for the first time, perfect examples of the very different kinds of stories I tell.

In this collection you'll find suspense, horror, and some tales just flat out weird and wooly. Please treat them like a box of chocolates and sample at will. Like your candy dark and bittersweet? Prefer nuts and chews? Whatever your taste, I hope you'll find something to your liking.

Maxine O'Callaghan
Lake Elsinore, California

A Change of Clients

I got to bed at two in the morning, too exhausted to resist the nightmare: a cliff lashed by wind-shattered sea spray, Dana Point glittering below, Jack walking into a trap . . .

The telephone jerked me awake, shaking and sweating.

"Wake up, Delilah," Rita chirped. "Got a live one for you."

After three days spent tracking a runaway through the L.A. jungles, I was in no mood for cheerfulness. I squinted against bright sunlight and muttered mild obscenities.

"Now, now," Rita reproved, "you want to be a successful female private eye, you gotta grab the clients when they come along. Write this down. Craig Zarath." She added an address and directions. "Be there at one o'clock and he says to bring a suitcase. It might take a few days."

"Rita, you know I like to see clients in my office."

She laughed. "Honeychile, you really are asleep. Zarath, I said—as in Zarath Construction. You have time to brush your teeth if you get moving."

"Here I thought I was on my own," I said nastily, "but actually I'm working for my answering service."

"I have to keep you on your toes or I don't get paid, speaking of which—"

"I'm going, I'm going."

I hung up the phone and rubbed aching temples. Every monotonous, ear-splitting hour of the previous night still throbbed, but at the least the dream was gone. I showered, swallowed aspirin and plugged in the percolator while I

9

packed, dressed and checked the contents of the leather bag that serves as briefcase and purse. Jack had given me the bag when we opened the agency.

Quickly, I suppressed memory and drank the stomach-jarring coffee. It helped. My head cleared a little as I drove west on the Newport Freeway and thought about Zarath Construction. I knew the company specialized in pseudo-Spanish subdivisions. From their proliferation in southern Orange County, I guessed the company was big and probably growing bigger.

Leaving the freeway, I followed Rita's directions toward the coastal hills to Zarath's house. The best California modern with angular lines that looked all glass, it blended into a wild hillside. The Pacific gleamed on the horizon. It was a safe bet that Zarath owned a chunk of surrounding land as a buffer against the urban sprawl he helped to create.

The driveway circled and offered parking beneath a second-story deck, mounted on massive concrete posts, that jutted over a deep ravine.

Taking a deep breath, I ordered myself to concentrate on the job. I sure wasn't adjusting to widowhood. West & West Detective Agency was just me now—regardless of what it said in faded gold leaf on the office door in Santa Ana.

A heavyset maid let me in, took me to the den and asked me to wait. I blinked and sat down. Against a wallpaper suggestive of tawny African veldts, big cats stalked the room in poster-size photographs: leopards snarled and unsheathed razor-sharp claws; a lion devoured the broken body of a gazelle.

My empty stomach quivered. I was grateful when Craig Zarath finally arrived, looking right at home with the rest of the predators. He had a hard body, sleek hair, a face dominated by a bony nose and black eyes that blended pupil with iris. I imagined him main-lining Essence of Chauvinism every day before breakfast.

He stood an inch too close and pressed my fingers while he said, "Delilah West."

Females usually dropped left and right, I presume, but I just sat down and waited politely.

Without wasting any more charm he said succinctly, "I want you to watch my wife."

"I don't take divorce cases—"

"It's not that. During the next week, I need somebody competent around because I'm afraid she may try to harm herself."

"Suicide? Why me? Sounds like a good nurse—"

"She'd spot one a mile away, and don't suggest commitment. Margaret's not insane."

"You have household help."

"Just Consuelo and she's only here half days. Well?"

At least it would be a change from unwashed bodies and acid rock, and considering the condition of my bank account I really couldn't afford to be choosy. Still, I stalled by asking, "Why are you particularly concerned about this week?"

"Two years ago my wife was involved in an automobile accident. She was driving; our infant son was killed. Naturally she blamed herself. She had a rough year and then when I thought she was pulling out of it she tried to drown herself. That was right around the anniversary of Jimmy's death. I simply don't want to chance another episode like last year. There's not a lot I can do but I would feel better if you were here to keep an eye on her."

"You seem to have a lot of confidence in me."

"I checked out your background. Swim team and gymnastics in college; policewoman; well-trained." His eyes did a complete job of assessment. "You look perfectly capable to

11

me—among other things. Half your fee now as a retainer, Mrs. West."

His idea of a retainer did a lot to blunt my curiosity. I took it and let him press my fingers again before he finished his briefing.

Ostensibly I was helping him at home with an overload of office work. He had form letters and reports as a cover. His assumption that I typed raised a few Lib-type hackles, but I bit my tongue.

"Margaret doesn't go out much these days," he told me. "If she does, follow her. Lord knows what she'll try."

"Any relatives? Friends?"

"No relatives except a few distant cousins. Since the accident, she's cut herself off from her friends."

Prickles of uneasiness had sprouted on the back of my neck. I didn't like any of this. Somehow Zarath impressed me as the type who didn't give a damn about anybody except himself. He looked past my left ear and said, "Margaret." I knew then that I was right. He didn't love his wife.

Tiny and gaunt, she had an unfocused look in her bruised eyes and dull brown hair curling around a thin face that remained sallow beneath a suntan.

"Margaret, you promised to take a nap." His voice was even but edged with ice.

"I can't sleep."

She was strung out on something; her unsteady beeline for the bar told me what. After a slug of vodka, she noticed me sitting there and horror twisted her face. "You brought her here," she whispered, "No, Craig—"

"Mrs. West is from the temporary agency," Zarath cut in smoothly.

Another jolt of vodka steadied her slightly. She tried to rearrange her face into a smile.

"Since my hours are going to be irregular," Zarath went on, "Mrs. West will stay here for a few days. Show her the guestroom, will you? I have to go to the construction site." His nod included both of us as he left.

Margaret took a pair of sunglasses from the pocket of her terry robe; it was a relief when her eyes were covered. "I didn't mean to be rude," she said shakily.

I said something reassuring but she wasn't listening. Her eyes fastened on the photograph of the lion and she seemed cold sober as she said, "I hate this room."

"The pictures are a bit scary," I agreed, "but good. Who's the photographer?"

"Craig. I suppose if he'd lived when big game hunting was fashionable he'd have mounted heads. Instead of that he hunts with a camera. Or else a tranquilizer gun. A friend of his works for the zoo and Craig goes collecting specimens with him. He talked me into going along once." She shivered at the memory and turned away. "Please excuse me, Mrs. West."

Any further attempt to get close to her was ended for the moment. I sighed and found Consuelo to ask about my room. It was next to Margaret's, sharing the deck that projected over the ravine.

I noted the drop down the boulder-strewn hillside and my apprehension grew. Obviously I couldn't be with Margaret every minute. She could slash her wrists, gulp a bottle of pills or blow her brains out—all with me in the next room. It was senseless for Zarath to hire me as a watchdog. I told myself it was his money.

Still the doubt nagged all afternoon as I did the feigned work and answered a few calls on Zarath's business line in the den. Once I managed to slip into Margaret's room. It confirmed my pessimism—bottles of sleeping pills, razor

13

blades—the only thing missing was a gun and I guessed there was one in the house somewhere.

I finally ran out of lame excuses to check on Margaret, and I paced the den feeling right at home with the feline menagerie.

Not for the first time did I ask myself what I was doing cooped up in a place I didn't want to be, worrying about people I didn't know. It was fun when Jack and I were a team, but now . . . I could go back on the police force, I suppose. I hear they even let women do something besides hand out parking tickets. Maybe . . .

While I brooded, Consuelo worked like a grim whirlwind and left after preparing dinner. Margaret paced her room—I assumed it was definitely her room; there was no sign of male occupation—or else she lay on the deck with her sunglasses pushed up across the top of her head and her face bared to the sun. Once I heard muffled crying through the door that stayed closed despite my efforts.

Dinner was something less than sparkling. Zarath made polite conversation, nothing more. Margaret drank steadily and her pale eyes watched him with despair.

I'd made up my mind by then that she needed a doctor more than a bodyguard and to hell with the fee. I told him so.

"I hired you to watch Margaret, not to give me advice," he said coldly. He was on his way out and I'd caught him with his hand on the doorknob. "Anyway, we've spent a fortune on psychiatrists. It didn't help."

I tried again. "Maybe if you took her away—"

"Impossible. Oh, look here, I'm not heartless but I've watched my wife degenerate from a lovely woman to the verge of alcoholism and suicide. Maybe you're right. It didn't work before, but as soon as I can manage it I'll take Margaret on a trip."

I ought to have been reassured but, as the kids say, the vibes were bad. I wandered restlessly around the house until a crash from Margaret's room sent me flying upstairs. She had tripped and fallen—not surprising considering her intake of alcohol that evening.

She mumbled her thanks as I helped her to the bed. "You're good to me, Delilah. I thought at first you and Craig—but I was wrong—that was somebody else. I *was* wrong?"

"Yes," I said firmly. "It's strictly business."

Tears slipped down her cheeks. "It was wonderful once; Craig loved me. We had a baby, did you know that? But he died and Craig—Craig never forgives."

"Mrs. Zarath, if you're unhappy maybe you should go away."

"Where would I go?"

"Mexico. Hawaii. Float around the world. Get back your health." Forget Craig Zarath, I wanted to add.

"I can't do that. I won't make it easy for him. I'm not going to give him up."

"What if he makes the break himself?" I asked brutally.

"Craig will never leave me."

"Won't he?"

She shook her head stubbornly. "He wouldn't. He can't. Go 'way now, leave me alone. I want to—go to sleep . . ."

With her words feeding my apprehension, I left her and went downstairs to call Rita. She said she thought she knew somebody—which didn't surprise me. Rita has more sources of information than the CIA—I can depend on her.

She called back an hour later. "When Zarath Construction incorporated, Craig and Margaret kept the majority of the stock in equal amounts. The rest was sold publicly to various investors."

15

"So Craig Zarath has the controlling interest as long as he votes his wife's share."

"Yep. It was Margaret's money originally, it seems. One interesting fact, Delilah. Somebody's buying up stock. I don't know who, just that it isn't your boy. Help any?"

"Yeah, Rita, thanks."

It didn't though. It explained why Zarath put up with a wife who lived like a zombie—he couldn't risk a divorce—but it didn't explain his concern over her survival. The fact was, he'd be better off with his wife dead.

I slept in snatches until Zarath slunk in about 1:00 a.m. The rest of the night I prowled the hall, stopped again and again to listen to Margaret's ragged breathing, and knew my vigil wasn't to protect Margaret from herself.

When sunrise clotted the fog and chased it out to sea, the primitive sense of danger quieted. I relaxed. It's instinctive to lower your guard once the terrors of night are over.

That's my excuse, but it doesn't help much. Warm, sunny mornings will haunt me for a long time.

The day began with Margaret stumbling down to make breakfast. Her hands shook and her eyes were hollow and sick. I drank coffee, chewed toast and studied Zarath. He ate, as he did everything, with controlled savagery. There was tension too; a pulse jumped in his temple and he kept looking at his watch. Still, when he caught my interest, his eyes gleamed with a speculation that made my skin crawl. I got up abruptly and began clearing the table before Margaret noticed.

"I didn't hear you come in last night, Craig." Her tentative words were soft. I wanted to shout: speak up, woman!

"The meeting ran late," Zarath said.

"Could we have a talk this morning? Please?"

"It will have to wait, darling. I'm meeting somebody. I

have a few things to go over with Mrs. West and then I'll be off." With a sudden show of tenderness he cupped Margaret's chin and kissed her. I felt cold. "Leave all this stuff for the maid, Maggie; go up and sit in the sun. It's a lovely day."

Her face lit and she nodded blindly. "Will you be home for dinner, Craig?" she asked hopefully.

He smiled, promising.

As soon as he went upstairs he motioned me into the den. "Watch her, Delilah." His face was grim. "The accident happened two years ago today."

"She seemed happy this morning."

"Perhaps. I hope you're right." He shuffled papers and stuffed some into his briefcase. Over his shoulder, the lion devoured his kill. "I'll come home as soon as I can. Stick close to her." He slapped his coat in annoyance. "I left my pen someplace. No, don't bother, I'll find it."

He was back quickly with Margaret's sunglasses in his hand. "She left these in the kitchen. Take them up, will you?"

He sounded almost as though he loved his wife, unless you remembered the sound of love in a man's voice. I remembered.

I decided to have another talk with Margaret. On the deck, she relaxed on a redwood chaise. Mexican pots of yellow daisies splashed sun colors even in the shade.

"Did Craig go? My sunglasses, I wonder where—"

"You left them in the kitchen." Absently she put them across her hair like a bandeau. "I brought coffee for us. Do you mind?" It seemed like a good excuse.

"Oh, thanks. I'd like that." The glow was still on her face; all it had taken was a few kind words from Zarath. His return to cold indifference would quickly snuff it out.

As I picked up the coffeepot, the telephone rang distantly.

"It's Craig's business line downstairs," Margaret said. "You'd better answer it."

17

One of Zarath's secretaries had a long message full of figures. "Can't this wait?" I asked irritably. Although Margaret was in good spirits, I still felt uneasy. I cut off the girl's indignant reply and her voice buzzed on and on. Only part of me wrote down her words. Inside I waited, straining to hear something other than silence, and then Margaret screamed.

As I threw down the phone and raced upstairs, her scream choked off. I pounded across the empty deck to the railing just as Zarath ran from the parking area under the deck and slid down the slope yelling her name.

Doctor, ambulance—my mind offered the frantic hope, but I already knew it was too late. I *knew* it as I ran from the house and skittered toward the blue blotch in the ravine. She lay with her head at a horrible angle. Blood formed a pool under the broken glasses beside her face and sunlight glittered in a mixture of redness and glass shards. Zarath crouched over her body.

"Is she—" I couldn't bear to touch the skinny wrist.

"Dead. She's dead. I decided to check through my briefcase and I saw her—where the hell were you? I told you to stay close."

"There was a phone call. She seemed all right."

"Seemed." He swore and started to pick her up.

"You'd better leave her there, Mr. Zarath." Despite my numbness, training clicked off a prescribed routine. "I'll call the police."

After that I lost track of time; official cars arrived. Zarath answered questions; I corroborated his answers. Yes, Mrs. Zarath was despondent. She drank too much. I knew she'd attempted suicide before. Zarath carefully made no remark about my dereliction of duty. Margaret's body was taken away and the police left with words of condolence to Craig Zarath.

He waited only long enough to speak to me. "I apologize for the things I said, Delilah. The shock, I suppose. I really shouldn't blame you. Margaret had made up her mind, so . . ." He got into his car and started the engine. "I'll send you a check for the balance of your fee."

I must have nodded. He drove away and left me standing there with all that blasted sunlight pouring over the golden hills. Averting my eyes from the ravine where Margaret's blood was soaking into the rocky earth, I headed for the bar in Zarath's den, gulped down brandy and stared at the pictures lining the walls.

For the first time I truly understood Margaret's aversion to the photographs. I looked at the lion ravaging the broken body of the gazelle and recognition raised an icy Braille of hackles on my neck. Out there in the ravine when Zarath lifted his head—for a split second that same feral victory blazed in his eyes.

He killed her.

I stood there, with his presence filling the room like animal scent, and knew it. What's more, he used me. Brought me here and lied to me and set me up as a witness. He killed her and he was going to get away with it unless I stopped him.

Gut-deep anger burned away the sickness that had paralyzed my judgment ever since I'd heard Margaret Zarath's dying scream. Zarath didn't know it but sometime during the night I'd stopped working for him and taken his wife for my client.

I poured more brandy and thought about Zarath's actions just before Margaret's death. He'd been in a hurry to leave but once outside he'd dithered around checking papers in his briefcase. So—why? If he'd heard the telephone and knew I was busy in the den, did he slip back inside and push his wife off the deck?

Well, he hadn't come in the front door—I had a view of it from the den—and even if he entered through the kitchen I was out of this room as soon as Margaret screamed. Which put him on the deck with only seconds to get down to the parking area.

I knew it was impossible, but I went up to the deck anyway. Given time and a rope he could have gone down the concrete pillars, I suppose. I'd bet money he hadn't. So, figure he was down there beneath the deck. After that touching moment at breakfast, if he'd called to her she'd have rushed over to the railing. I gripped the solid barrier and looked down—as Margaret must have looked. If he called from the shadows beneath the deck, she'd lean over, far over. My hands grew slimy with sweat as I tried to crawl back in time. Had he counted on her simply falling?

Would a lion expect the gazelle to trip and break its neck? Neither would Zarath. A weapon, then. Not a gun meant to kill; this was to be suicide. A tranquilizer gun.

It fit.

I had a hazy idea from television that a gun like that makes a minimum of noise. At any rate, the only thing I'd heard was Margaret's scream. I'd never forget it. I remembered exactly: it was not drawn out, not wavering and falling in the peculiar echo of a cry going away down through space, but choking off. In the silence there were other sounds: a sliding hiss of fabric over wood and the final thump of a body striking rock. The pattern made sense if she'd been unconscious when she fell.

If Zarath planned a hiding place for the gun close by, he could figure on getting to the body and removing the dart before I saw it. His car was the logical place; but by now the gun, along with dart, would be somewhere below salt water.

It made sense except for one thing. Why did Zarath take it

for granted that Margaret would freeze and give him a clear shot? If she'd seen him standing there aiming a gun at her, wouldn't she jump back instinctively? *If she'd seen him.* That was the question.

For the second time that day I ran out of the house and down the slope. The sunglasses marked the spot where Margaret had fallen. Both lenses were cracked. One was intact; the other partially knocked out. I remembered Zarath handing them to me to take to her and Margaret absently slipping them across her hair. When Zarath called, she would have slid them down on her nose. I'd seen her do it yesterday.

My hands shook as I picked them up. The cracked lens stayed in place. My stomach lurched as my beautiful theory fell to pieces like the shards of glass littering the ground.

I felt like banging my head against the rock with frustration. Would the autopsy turn up the drug?

Instinctively, I knew he'd plan for that and use something untraceable. There would be a mark where the dart entered her body. Enough evidence . . . maybe. But Zarath had laid his groundwork carefully. I could hear his attorney asking: "Why would Margaret Zarath stand there and let her husband shoot her?" The whole thing was sufficiently bizarre to plant doubt in a jury's mind.

Although I was stymied, I went inside for an envelope and picked up the pieces of glass with their rusty coating of dried blood. In the den I spread them out on Zarath's desk like a dark jigsaw puzzle.

The answer was there as I suspected.

I made two phone calls. One confirmed the only thing left to nag me. My voice still retained enough official bluster to find out that Zarath's secretary had been instructed to call at precisely ten o'clock.

Drained, I stood up to go pack my bag, but outside wheels

21

crunched on gravel. I sat back down and waited for Zarath.

He must have read my face but he chose to bluff it out and contemptuously ignored the litter of glass.

"I thought you'd gone, Delilah. Margaret's dead. You lost your job when you let her jump and break her neck."

"I'm not buying it anymore. I know you killed her."

He came across the room, catlike, and leaned over me. "Be very careful, Delilah. The police don't want guesses. They want proof."

"It was clever," I admitted, "and all carefully timed. That phone call, for instance. It kept me far enough away so I couldn't be sure of what I heard. The only variable was the weather. I suppose you'd simply have postponed things if it hadn't been sunny enough for her to be on the deck. But she was and—tell me, Mr. Zarath, was she really dead when you got to her or did you have to finish the job?"

"She was dead, all right; you saw for yourself."

"I imagine it simplified things for you. As it was you were very busy. You had to hide the gun, get to her before I did and remove the tranquilizer dart. And then there were the glasses."

"You really are reaching, Delilah."

"Margaret was nearsighted, but vain enough to wear only prescription *sunglasses*. I should have realized yesterday, when she thought I was somebody else. You switched the glasses this morning. When she looked down at you from the deck you were a myopic blur. She didn't know you had a gun in your hands. After she fell, you simply switched them back with a quick crack against a rock to make the prescription pair look realistic. I admit it threw me off—until I realized there were too many pieces of glass. The other pair shattered badly in the fall, didn't they? You put the frames in your pocket but you couldn't hide the broken glass just then; it was a bloody

22

mess. I suspect you'd have gone down later to tidy up."

He moved fast, slid open the right-hand drawer of the desk and came up with a gun, not a tranquilizer gun but a very efficient-looking revolver.

"It sounds weak, Delilah. Very weak. But I can't take the chance of your babbling it, can I?"

"Oh, don't be an ass," I said wearily. "I've already called the police."

I'd talked long enough. We both heard the car outside and the authoritative knocking. I stood up deliberately and walked to the door. My insides quivered but when I turned he stood there with the gun dangling uselessly. Behind him, the lion stared at me with arrogant fierceness.

The cat didn't remind me of Craig Zarath anymore.

Bad News

Like cancer specialists and termite inspectors, PIs often are hired to tell people things they don't want to hear. So I was doing my job, personally delivering a videotape that confirmed my client's worse suspicions about her husband.

This is not a part of the work that I enjoy. To make matters worse, Julie Haverson wanted me to drive over to Palm Springs with my report, and she was paying too much money for me to say no.

It was a Friday in mid June. Forget that "what is so rare" stuff. Obviously the guy who wrote the poem never spent much time in L.A. where June weather means that sullen morning clouds hang around most days until late afternoon.

From the looks of I-10 everybody in the L.A. basin had picked up and headed for the desert. In addition to cars and semis, the road was bumper to bumper with RVs, jeeps, motorcycles, and pickups towing trailers loaded with an assortment of boats, dune buggies, and dirt bikes. We crept down from Banning past rank upon rank of huge windmills lining the sere brown hills along the interstate like something out of Jules Verne. On the radio a disc jockey announced smugly that it was 117 degrees at three o'clock. Even the sky looked hot. I counted five dust devils whirling through the sand and cactus.

I was cool enough in my metal cocoon. The Astrovan has both front and rear air conditioners. If necessary the powerful unit in back could bring the temperature down low enough to set up a temporary meat locker. Still, call me a pessimist, but

24

in the desert I can't help but feel that I am only a broken radiator hose away from being buzzard bait and bleached bones.

I picked up the car phone and dialed Julie's number to let her know about the delay. I'd tried to reach her earlier, only to catch the answering machine; now, I got it again. It would be my luck to drive all the way out here to find she'd forgotten our appointment and was headed back to the coast.

Our first meeting was a week ago today in Newport Beach. We had sat across from each other on two huge couches in a room built to take in the view of the Back Bay through a good thirty feet of windows. Beyond an expanse of lawn, a high wrought-iron fence, and a margin of tidal marsh, the water was gunmetal gray under low, gloomy clouds.

We got the introductions out of the way, agreeing on Delilah and Julie, although the informality didn't seem to put either of us at ease.

Julie was my age—mid-thirties. Her cream-colored silk shirt cost more than my entire outfit. She wore this tucked into an ancient brown corduroy skirt; there were brown leather flats on her feet, small diamond studs in her ears.

I took a sip of the coffee she had served and put the cup down carefully on the low table between us. Obviously Julie wasn't used to children, dogs, or clumsy PIs. The couches were oyster white; everything else was light beige or pale gray except for an Oriental rug in rich reds that looked as though it had been spun from silk. The rest of the furniture was antiques, graceful curving shapes and wood that had that unmistakable patina of age and value.

"Neal and I have been married for two years," Julie began. "And we've been happy, much happier than I ever expected to be. I don't flatter myself, Delilah. My father began telling me at an early age that I'd never be much to look at, but I'd still have lots of men chasing me for my money."

25

She missed being homely by virtue of a good orthodontist and a great hairdresser. She didn't smile often but when she did her teeth were small, white, and even. Coppery highlights glinted in the straight brown bob. With some makeup, a new wardrobe—face it, she'd still be a woman people described as having very nice eyes.

Men have told me I'm beautiful and once or twice I believed it. With her memory of her father's words, I suspected poor Julie never would.

"This is your first marriage?" I asked.

"For both of us."

"So what happened?"

"Nothing much at first." She stared down into her bone china cup. "Neal just gradually became so—so distant."

Which meant, I assumed, the sex had cooled considerably. Then there had been phone calls at odd hours, a charge card slip from an intimate little restaurant down in Laguna that Neal tried to pass off as a business expense.

"You could ask him about it," I said. "There might be a simple explanation." Understand I didn't really believe this; my profession makes me cynical on the subject of fidelity. Still, it seemed a tactful thing to say.

"I've tried to talk to him," Julie said. "But I can never find the right words. Because I'm afraid—what if I'm wrong? He would be so hurt, he might never forgive me."

From the anguish on her face, I knew that whatever he was, whatever he'd done, she loved the guy.

"You'd better think about this," I warned. "Are you sure you really want to know?"

"I have to. He made me believe he really loved me. If that's a lie . . ." She had put down her coffee and picked up her checkbook, her eyes like flint. "Do what you have to do, Delilah. I need to know the truth."

No, there was no way Julie Haverson had changed her mind.

Following Julie's instructions I exited the interstate at Bob Hope Drive and found my way to her street. The town looked torpid and heat-stunned under a brassy sky. Very few people were actually outside the life support bubble of their cars. I saw one old guy on a bicycle, a heart attack waiting to happen.

Julie had come out to the desert because she said the lack of sunlight triggered bouts of depression for her, and she was depressed enough about Neal. She also wanted to provide hubby with enough rope and give me a chance to set up the hanging.

Pretty soon the houses thinned out; up long driveways, these were white stucco, built low to hug the earth and hide under Mexican fan palms and tamarisk. The street dipped down into arroyos, places where you would not want to be caught during one of the wild winter storms that blow in off the Baja. I drove slowly, trying to read numbers off mailboxes.

According to my count the next one was Julie's—the house with squad cars and a coroner's van on the driveway. No mistake, the mailbox said *Haverson*. Dread crowded my throat as I parked and got out. A uniformed officer came to meet me and tell me the news. My client wasn't going to have to hear about her husband's dirty little secrets after all.

The coroner and the forensics crew were county. Since Julie's house was located in Desert Edge, not Palm Springs, the cops were local. Chief Frank Krause was a lanky, knobby man with a flap of belly hanging over his belt. A tan Stetson covered a head that was bald except for a fringe of gray hair. The Stetson was off and lying on a patio table. We sat on cushioned lawn chairs in the shade and sweated. The body had just been removed from the house, the doors and windows opened to air the place out.

"You all right?" Krause asked.

I nodded, but to tell the truth it would be a while before I forgot the sight of Julie Haverson's pale, bloated body. She had been found in a full bathtub of water, but she was already being bagged when I saw her.

"Who found her?" I asked.

"One of my people. A neighbor called us."

"How long has she been dead?"

"Coroner won't commit himself, but it had to be several days. When's the last time you talked to her?"

"Last Friday. A week ago today."

She had told me there was no need for interim reports before our appointment. She said she'd like to hear it from me personally if the news was good or bad. The only time I'd tried to call was from the car phone on the way over, and I'd had no reason to suspect anything was wrong when she didn't answer.

"Do you know the cause of death yet?" I asked.

"Not yet." Krause seemed content to answer my questions, watching me all the while like a canny old desert tortoise. "Well, you saw her. Not easy to call, but she was flat on her back in the tub. Doors were locked. No sign of a break-in. Looked to me like she slipped and drowned. Then you show up, and I find out she hired herself a private detective. What you were doing for her—you think it had something to do with her death?"

"Could be."

I hesitated. In my profession, cops are not always the enemy, but they are usually not your buddies. So what I was about to do went strictly against the grain. Still, Krause seemed a good man, and if there was any question about the way Julie died, there were things I wanted him to know.

"Chief," I said, "you and I need to watch some television."

Photographs are one thing, but nothing's as effective as video. Ask anybody who saw the tape of L.A.'s Finest beating up a suspect. My camera of choice used to be a fine old Nikon that belonged to my husband Jack. Since I often screwed up the f-stops and the focus, the pictures I produced were usually blurred and marginally acceptable.

My assistant, Danny Thu, has updated my office introducing me to computers and camcorders. Danny works for me part-time while finishing a double major in business and computer science at UC Irvine. I left the selection in his capable hands and he picked out a video camera that is small and idiot-proof with auto focus, low-light sensitivity, and a high-power zoom lens.

So when Frank Krause and I settled down in his spacious office, where he had not only a television set and a VCR but a couple of comfortable chairs as well, the picture was first-class.

The time and date, registered down in one corner of the frame, shows that I started to tape Neal Haverson's movements on Monday morning at 8:25 a.m. Neal had been out here in Desert Edge over the weekend. I pick him up as the garage door hums open at the house in Newport Beach and his green Porsche backs out. There's just a glimpse of dark hair and wraparound shades until we cut to him unfolding his lean body as he exits the car in the parking lot at Burdick, Fenster and Robb.

According to Danny this firm of stockbrokers is reputable but not big-time. It's also Danny's opinion that serious brokers get to work very early, about the time the market opens in New York. Maybe they keep Neal around for decoration. He has the kind of good looks that are a little too planned for my tastes. The perfect tan, a mouth that crooks easily into a charming smile. No wonder Julie fell for the guy. Me, I'm just the suspicious type.

After the intro there was a minimum of boring footage mixed in with the highlights. A waste of tape to record the man's every action. In-camera editing, Danny calls it. Anyway, there was a complete log, too, of course. I hadn't done the surveillance solo. I explained to Julie I'd need another operative, maybe more if one of us was made. She didn't quibble over the expense. A friend of mine who works out of Long Beach took the first shift; I took the second, and Danny relieved us when necessary. Either we were lucky or Neal was oblivious because he didn't spot any of us.

The very first day Neal leaves the office at 12:10 p.m. and drives over to another building in the commercial complex. A woman stands there waiting, greyhound-thin with full breasts, a long straight fall of tawny hair. She's so perfect you have to wonder how much she owes to plastic surgery. A red miniskirt shows off her legs as she gets into the Porsche. Old Neal was nothing if not predictable.

We cut to the two of them going into that same restaurant in Laguna where Neal indiscreetly charged a meal, Neal's hand resting in casual intimacy on the small of the woman's back.

They adjourn to their respective offices for a few hours of work, then meet for dinner and go on to her place, the activity behind the closed mini-blinds unrecorded but easily imagined. When Krause asked I told him the blonde's name was Suzanne Valco. He expressed no interest in the details of how I knew that, and I was just as glad not to have to explain, the rules about DMV access in California being what they are.

Suzanne was the only woman Neal was seeing, at least that week, but he saw her a lot. And at some of the most expensive bistros and dives Orange County had to offer. While following them around, I ate well, drank a lot of fizzy, non-alcoholic drinks, and listened to too much loud rock music. I might never have a club soda or play the radio again.

The highlight of the surveillance tape came on Thursday, last night, when Neal took his lover home to the house in Newport Beach. Julie's house. I thought about stopping the taping and claiming I had lost Neal, but my client was paying to know the worst. Who was I to censor the material?

After Neal and Suzanne went inside, I sat in my van, having a few dark thoughts about the amount of sleaze I have to witness and wondering what that sleaze was doing to my moral fiber. There's plenty of time to brood on a stakeout. The only alternative is booze, which I've managed to avoid, at least while sitting around in parked cars. So I settled in for a good long spell of introspection, but just then the lights came on in the backyard. I could see the glow on the trees, mostly off to the right side of the house, one palm lit up as though a spotlight was focused on it.

I recalled sitting with Julie, looking out toward the Back Bay, and remembered glimpsing a pool and a spa off on the right side, maybe placed so as not to interrupt the view of the bay or perhaps just situated for privacy.

I hesitated, sighed, then dug out a small flashlight, picked up the video camera, and climbed out of the van. Taping a person's actions is a very sticky situation these days with the possibility of lawsuits always a consideration. The basic rule is you can't stand on private property to point your camera. While I confess to cutting a corner or two, one may as well go along with the legal niceties whenever possible, and I was in luck because along the pool side of the Haversons' backyard ran a convenient strip of public land providing access to the Back Bay.

My flashlight is a very dim hooded light, perfect for car burglars and other nefarious characters like me. Good thing I'd brought it along because it was damn dark with not a spark of starlight penetrating the overcast and very little spillover from the street lamps. I could hear laughter and the sounds of bubbling water and a pool pump as I picked my way along a graveled path through head-high thorny shrubs to a big old acacia tree. It had been a while since my tomboy youth, but my jeans and Nikes were perfect for climbing. A thick sturdy branch provided an unobstructed view, especially when I used the zoom lens.

The angle was perfect, looking down into the spa, and with the lights in the water and more lights in the shrubbery, you could see everything those two naked, slippery bodies were doing.

Krause sat silently for a moment as that last scene ended, watching the screen dance with electronic snow.

"I didn't think Julie needed to see any more than that," I said.

Krause reached over to turn off the television. "Man's a real piece of work."

"He may be a murderer as well."

Krause gave a noncommittal grunt. "Lots of guys cheat on their wives."

"Lots of guys kill them, too."

"Most don't."

"Most don't have wives as rich as Julie Haverson. Look, maybe he suspected Julie knew about his affair. Maybe he was tired of her anyway and figured it was only a matter of time until she divorced him."

"And maybe his wife died while you were dogging his every footstep, so he has an alibi."

"I didn't do a twenty-four-hour on him," I said. "I tucked him in and my other operative picked him up in the morning. He had all night to come over here."

"Yeah, well, it's three hours round trip plus whatever time it took to do the job. Man looked awful bright-eyed to me every time he went off to work." Krause got up and went over to eject the tape. "Anyway, it's all speculation until the coroner tells us how and when Mrs. Haverson died." He held up the videocassette. "You mind if I keep this for now?"

"Be my guest."

The original was back in my office. I noticed Krause hadn't questioned whether the tape would be admissible if and when Neal was ever charged. I hoped that meant he respected my professionalism but thought it more likely he figured he'd never have to use the tape as evidence.

"Have they scheduled the autopsy?" I asked.

"There wasn't any hurry before. But now—"

He broke off as his intercom buzzed, went to his desk to pick up the phone, listened, said, "Okay, I'll be right there." To me he said, "Haverson's here." Krause tilted his head toward the door, and I saw Julie's husband through the glass, waiting outside.

It was Neal, all right. I'd know him anywhere, with or without clothes. He looked sober and jumpy, a little pale under the tan. A natural reaction to traumatic news, or just a case of guilt and nerves?

"I'm going to push for the postmortem right away," Krause said. "In case we need a statement, you going on back to the coast tonight?"

I wanted to sleep in my own bed and wake up tomorrow to

a cool, damp June morning. But I also badly needed a stiff drink, a shower, and, eventually, food. Well, after reviewing the tape and seeing Neal Haverson out there, I thought I could use more than one drink and then I ought not to be driving. I told Krause I'd stay overnight in the area, that I'd call his office when I checked in.

He promised to let me know as soon as he had the autopsy results, put the cassette in his desk drawer, and picked up the phone to tell the officer who acted as receptionist to send Haverson in.

Neal held the door for me on my way out, giving me the once-over as I went past. The flicker of interest in his eyes was pure reflex. He didn't recognize me. He was just doing a quick evaluation and registering approval. And never mind that his wife was in the morgue. My reaction was instantaneous and came strictly from my gut, not my head. I *knew*, all the same.

The son of a bitch had killed his wife.

The Ocotillo Lodge was a nice little motel that didn't bill itself as a luxurious resort. It was clean and moderately priced, with a restaurant next door, the Baja Grill, which specialized in fish tacos. The margaritas were huge, frosty, and potent. I had one as soon as I sat down and another while I ate. Homemade tortillas, fish grilled over mesquite, fresh, chunky salsa.

I managed to put off thinking about Julie's death until I got back to my room and crawled into bed. What I thought was that I ought to be a little careful here. Jumping to intuitive conclusions was the easy part; proving that Neal was a killer was something else again. Furthermore, this wasn't my case. Julie had hired me to get the goods on her husband, and I had certainly done that. Look at it that way, my job was finished. And Frank Krause seemed a competent man. Let him take it from here.

Yeah.

Yeah, but—

What is it with me? Why do I have this little tic of moral obligation that I can't ignore? I hadn't even liked Julie very much. Not that I disliked her. We simply hadn't connected on a personal level. That wasn't unusual. I don't care much for a lot of my clients. But I do care when they wind up dead. And it bothered me that Julie had paid for her husband's alibi. It bothered me a lot.

I punched my pillow, tried to get comfortable in the unfamiliar bed, and listened to the air conditioner buzz.

My father was a cop for twenty years. He used to say that 99% of homicides were totally senseless and usually took place under the influence of drugs or alcohol. Say Julie had been the victim of some random nut case, her death might easily fall into that majority—always assuming she hadn't died accidentally. I didn't think so, but my hunches wouldn't mean spit in a court of law.

Money was at the top of the list for that small percentage of motivated crimes, closely followed by jealousy and lust. Neal rang most of the big bells. But one thing bothered me and was certain to bother twelve ordinary people who might have to decide Neal's guilt. Could he have killed his wife, then gone off to the fun week I'd recorded without showing any stress, anxiety, or guilt?

I remembered a recent news story. Two men kidnapped a young boy on his way home from McDonald's. They tortured and murdered the child—then one of them ate his burgers and fries for lunch.

Not only did I think Neal was capable of murdering his wife and then acting as though nothing had happened, I

35

thought that's exactly what he'd done. Now, the question was: Had he gone on with business as usual, figuring that was the best way to put doubt into the mind of any potential jury? Was the man an amoral monster, incapable of remorse?

The possibility guaranteed some mighty unpleasant dreams.

Morning sunlight lasered in through an opening where the drapes didn't quite meet, a wake-up call impossible to ignore. The inside of my nose burned from the dry air, and pain jabbed at my right temple. Not quite a hangover, but close enough.

I keep an overnight bag in the van, packed with basic necessities. Good thing, since the Ocotillo was short on amenities. I had just gotten out of the shower and was toweling my hair when Frank Krause called.

"Julie Haverson drowned," he said without much preamble. "Doc found a bruise where she hit the back of her head on the faucet, so it was just the way it seemed: She slipped, banged her head hard enough to knock herself out, and slid down in the water."

"And this happened when?"

"Monday or Tuesday, according to Doc. Definitely not Sunday."

"So that's it then?" I sat on the edge of the bed with cold water dripping down my back. "You're calling it an accident?"

"I'm calling it the way it is," he said wearily. "Look, I don't like the guy any more than you do, but the fact is Mrs. Haverson died after her husband left here last Sunday night. And even if there was any suspicion of foul play, we both know for the rest of the week—sixteen, seventeen hours a day—he had a perfect alibi."

He didn't have to remind me who was supplying that alibi.

"If it makes you feel any better," he added, "after the autopsy, I came back here and went over the reports. Went over everything. Hell, I haven't even been to bed yet. Take my word, Mrs. West, there's nothing there. My advice: Stop by for your videotape and then get out of this heat and go on home."

He said he was going home himself, that a man his age had no business staying up all night. If ever I was back in Desert Edge, be sure to come say hello.

And that was that.

Except that after we hung up I kept going over what he'd told me while I dressed and dried my hair. And logic and postmortem findings be damned, I was still convinced Neal had killed Julie.

And now it looked like the bastard was going to get away with it.

What people always say about the desert heat is that oh, yeah, it's hot all right, but it's *dry*. Yes, indeedy. Like somebody stuck you in one of those dehydrating ovens, the kind that turns juicy apricots into fruit leather. Walking from my van into the Desert Edge police station, I felt as if I was wearing heavy wool instead of my short-sleeved cotton shirt and jeans.

Inside, I saw only three officers, and one of them was heading out the back door as I came in. Another sat at a desk in a back corner, smoking and talking on the telephone. The third was the same woman who had served as receptionist the day before, Officer Noonan, according to her ID badge. She was thumbing through a stack of paperwork, looking as though she wished she was elsewhere. The radio on her desk was turned down and registered mostly static. A slow weekend. I wondered if they were all like that out here.

Noonan remembered me. When I asked for the videotape, she looked puzzled for a second, then said, "Oh, yeah, the Chief did say he was leaving it, but then we started talking about the report on Mrs. Haverson, and I guess he forgot. Why don't I have him mail it to you?"

"It's sensitive material," I said. "I'd really like to take it with me. Could you take a look in his office? My name's on the label."

"Well—"

"I certainly would appreciate it."

She nodded and stood up. "Do you know where he put it?"

There was a stack of file folders in her IN tray. The top one was marked Julie Haverson. What the hell—I hadn't made any plans for the weekend anyway.

"Gee," I said, "let me think. Maybe in that big file cabinet—the one over by the TV." The one I knew did not contain the tape.

As soon as she was gone, I positioned myself to block the view of the male cop who was still talking on the phone and flipped open the Haverson file. Pictures of Julie's bloated face made me glad I'd skipped breakfast. I scanned the coroner's report. Description of the bruise, measurement of the faucet. Major factors in estimating time of death: temperature of the house (an energy-conscious 78 degrees), temperature of the bath water, and the state of putrefaction. No help there.

Three witnesses. Of course, Krause hadn't exactly been beating the bushes. I noted names, speed-read their statements. No time to go over what Neal Haverson had said. I saw Noonan heading for Krause's desk, glancing out at me. I just stood there, trying to look innocent and hoping she wouldn't notice my reading material. She bent down to open

Krause's desk drawer, and I quickly closed the file folder.

When she came out of the Chief's office with my cassette, she gave me the once-over. She knew I was up to something, she just didn't know what. I thanked her and got the hell out of there before she figured it out.

"Had it to do over, I'd mind my own business," Henry Volsted said. "People pounding on my door, asking me questions."

Julie's next-door neighbor was a sawed-off little man who looked as though he'd been carrying a grudge of one kind or another for his entire seventy years. He was almost bald, his scalp tanned to a walnut brown. His face was the same shade and so were the scrawny arms and legs bared by madras plaid shorts and a yellow polo shirt. By contrast his wife Eileen was so pale I wondered if she ever went outside the house in daylight.

When Eileen had opened the door I'd managed to talk my way inside by saying I was a friend of Julie's, that I'd arrived for a visit yesterday only to find her dead. And I'd barged on into the living room before Henry arrived. A sofa and two chairs were upholstered in pale green damask, the curved backs outlined with fruitwood. The refrigerated air held a lingering smell of lemon furniture polish.

Dozens of small china figurines covered tabletops, the kind of knickknacks that are too expensive to trust to the hired help to dust. Maybe that's what kept Eileen inside.

"I am sorry to bother you like this," I said. "It was just so awful, driving up and seeing all the police cars, such a shock."

I sank down in a wing-backed side chair as though my knees had given way.

"Are you all right?" Eileen asked.

"I think it's the heat," I said. "Maybe some water . . ."

She nodded and scurried off while Henry jammed his hands in his pockets and glowered down at me.

"I keep thinking if only I'd come sooner—" I broke off to accept a glass from Eileen and sip.

"Oh, I don't know if it would've helped," Eileen said. "She was dead for days, wasn't she, Henry? Best to put it out of your mind and not brood about it."

"I know you're right," I said. "I just thought it might help to talk to people who knew her."

"Then you're in the wrong place," Henry said. "We keep to ourselves, and everybody else does the same. You're such a good friend, how come you're not talking to the husband?"

I explained that I didn't know Neal, that I'd met Julie through some charity work. "He should be grateful to you. Imagine if he'd come home and found Julie like that. What made you suspect something was wrong?"

I knew approximately what had happened from my quick perusal of Krause's file, but I wanted to hear it from them.

"Well, it was the Tremont delivery," Eileen said.

Tremont's, I recalled from the file, was a local grocery store. Julie had called them on Saturday to place an order with instructions for a delivery that day and another one mid-week.

"That was late Wednesday," Eileen went on. "I said it was funny, didn't I, Henry?—Julie not answering the door and her car sitting right there in the carport. I said maybe she was in the bathroom." Eileen faltered, looking stricken at her prophetic words. "The delivery boy left the box. I said it was awful, didn't I, Henry?—leaving stuff out in the heat like that. Well, we were gone most of Thursday. I didn't think anything, to tell the truth, until we got home. Then I saw the box was still sitting there. I had a feeling something was wrong—"

She glanced at her husband and got a venomous look in return. I could imagine Henry's response to her worry.

"I had Julie's number written down. For emergencies," Eileen added hastily, least I think she might ever call people just to be neighborly. "All I got was the answering machine. Henry kept saying her husband must've come and they went off somewhere and forgot about the delivery."

"As a matter of fact," I said, "Julie told me Neal might come back out one evening, maybe Monday or Tuesday."

"Well, he didn't," Eileen said positively. "I would have seen him."

Henry snorted. "What got us into this mess," he muttered. "Minding other people's business."

Another day before they finally called the police.

"I guess it didn't really matter that we waited so long, did it, Henry?" Eileen said. "Nobody could help Julie anyway."

Eileen Volsted might not have seen Neal on Monday or Tuesday night, but that didn't mean he hadn't been here. She had to sleep sometime. Come to that, he could have parked his car elsewhere and walked in. He wasn't invisible. Somebody would have seen him. But with the sun climbing up toward a blistering high noon, I delayed the canvass of the neighborhood and went to Tremont's instead.

I found the delivery boy, Johnny Torres, making up an order in the produce department, glancing nervously at a man who was spraying water on the romaine and bok choy. Torres was young and scared and the more questions I asked the more he lapsed into Spanish. I could understand enough to figure out he'd made both deliveries to the Haversons'. The first time, on Saturday, Julie was there. She signed the receipt and gave him a tip. But Wednesday, no. Nobody there. He saw nothing. *Nada.*

"Por favor," he said. He was very late, his boss would be angry.

41

I let him go. I hadn't expected much, but it was disappointing all the same. I stood there for a second, dreading going back out into the heat, breathing in the cool, earthy smell of carrots and potatoes.

The man who was spraying the vegetables had worked his way to the opposite end of the long greenery-laden counter. Another man joined him there; they spoke briefly, then ambled down toward me.

They were both in their forties. They wore tan wash-and-wear pants and green knit shirts with a logo: a tree sprouting up in the middle of the Tremont name. The produce man was a little taller and stockier and he had on a light green apron. The other one had a soft full mustache and had a plastic badge that said Manager pinned to his shirt.

"Heard you talking to Torres," the produce man said.

"The cops already questioned him," the manager said, pleasantly enough. "What's the deal?"

"Insurance investigation," was my quick lie.

"Mrs. Haverson's death was an accident, wasn't it?"

"More than likely."

It occurred to me that these two were the curious type who might pick up a wealth of information about their customers, but mostly I was stalling because I wasn't looking forward to going door to door in the hot sun, trying to find out something from the rest of Julie's neighbors.

"Mrs. Haverson had a large policy with us," I confided, "so we like to check things out. Did either of you know the Haversons?"

"Just to talk to on the phone—her, I mean. Never talked to him. How about you, Rick?" the manager said.

"Not that I know of. Of course my memory might improve if I could put my feet up and have a nice cold soda."

"Oh, yeah," the manager said. "Everybody knows a Coke

does wonders for the memory." He winked at me. "The stuff this guy will say just to take a break."

By this time I figured that a conversation with these two guys would come up goose eggs, but what the hell, I was also thirsty, so I went along with them back to the staff room, on a first-name basis by the time we arrived. The manager was Ray, Ray Tremont, who said, "I run the place until my dad gets tired of his golf game and shows up."

The crowded staff room held lockers, shelves, a long table, and some kitchen space furnished with a refrigerator and a microwave. The place smelled of popcorn and pizza. Rick took off his apron, sat on a brown plastic chair, and propped his feet on another one while Ray got cans of pop from the fridge. They kept up a running banter as I sipped my icy cola and thought that all I would accomplish here was to provide an audience for their good-natured standup routine.

"Do you get a lot of delivery orders?" I asked, casting about for some crumb of information.

"Lots of rich people in Desert Edge," Rick said. "They got better things to do than grocery-shop."

Ray said he took the orders, and that Julie had called hers in herself.

"Do you remember what she said?"

The two exchanged a look like I'd asked the jackpot question.

"She asked for sourdough bread, sliced turkey, lamb chops—" Ray rattled off a dozen more items.

"That was for Saturday," Rick said.

"She wanted extra fruit on Wednesday."

"We carry tree-ripened peaches. They spoil quick."

"Peaches, apricots, raspberries, two cartons of plain yogurt."

Rick grinned in admiration. "Photographic memory."

"A curse," Ray said modestly. "Imagine all the old grocery lists I got stored in my brain."

"What else did Mrs. Haverson say—besides giving her order?"

"Just hello and thank you."

Well, what would she have said? *Gotta run—my husband's filling the tub so he can drown me?*

Rick and Ray looked disappointed when I said I had to get going and thanked them for the drink. "And please tell Johnny Torres I didn't mean to get him in trouble. He isn't, is he?"

"Nah," Ray said. "Dumb to leave stuff in the sun, but what the heck, things happen."

"Screw-ups," Rick said.

He put his apron back on, and they walked me out, laughing about a major screw-up the weekend before.

"A party," Rick said. "All kinds of booze and food—"

"Deluxe catering tray from the deli," Ray recited on cue. "Buffalo wings, blue corn chips, fresh salsa, the works."

"Everything's been set aside ahead of time, of course, except—major botch—"

We were back out in the store by then. Freezer section. Rick pointed to a whole cabinet full of ice cubes in clear plastic and said, "Guess what?"

"Must have been a run on the stuff," Ray said. "All we had left was two bags."

"And ten cases of beer and wine coolers."

"Five cases of Michelob and five Seagrams Mixed Tropicals."

"They put it in tubs or coolers."

"Wanted ten bags."

"We ran all over town. Everybody was short."

"Better believe we laid in plenty this weekend."

"Ice."

They looked at each other and laughed.

I felt a little giddy myself, as if they'd just announced that I'd picked the winner in lotto.

Ice.

I had a very busy afternoon. At five-thirty I was sitting in a little park in downtown Desert Edge, wearing a tank top and a denim skirt, watching the sun slide behind the purple flanks of the Santa Rosa Mountains from a wooden bench that felt as though it belonged in a sauna. A breeze carried a strong scent of drying brush overlaid with the smell of melting asphalt. The temperature was down a few degrees although the sky still glowed bright and hot overhead.

Most people were off having frosty drinks in cool, dim bars. Only a couple of tourists braved the heat, one of them across the park capturing a cactus garden on video. Out on the street, Neal's green Porsche wheeled into a parking space, and he climbed out.

I'd found him easily enough. Not at the house. Bad vibes, I guess. Anyway, he could afford to stay elsewhere. I guessed it would be at one of the most expensive resorts in the area and found where he was registered on the second call. He must have received my messengered surprise.

I stood up and waved. He came over, stopped in front of me. The smooth charm had vanished. With that much fury twisting his face Neal wasn't even good-looking.

"You," he said. "You were in Krause's office yesterday."

"Watching a little TV."

"Shit."

His hands were balled into fists and he was menacingly close even if we were in a public place. I stepped back a pace and slipped my little Beretta mini-automatic from my skirt pocket, making sure he saw it.

He stayed where he was. "I don't care if Julie hired you," he said, suppressing his rage. "What you did was an invasion of my privacy. I called my lawyer, and I can sue your ass."

"One can always sue," I agreed. "Of course, then the tape would be made public."

"All right, let's get to it. What do you want?"

"Just to talk. To tell you I know how you tricked the coroner."

"What?" He stared at me. "You're crazy. I didn't do anything."

"Sure you did. After Julie drowned, you drained out the warm water—"

He stood very still, sweat shining on his face.

"Then," I said. "You put ice in the tub."

He had turned to stone. I began to wish I had Rick from Tremont's around to play second banana and fill in some details.

"I don't think you just piled it in," I said. "You probably worried about frostbite. So you took it slow, ran some cool water and kept putting in the ice. I imagine it took a while and a lot of the stuff."

"That's—that's ridiculous."

"I've got four clerks who remember you, Neal." Danny had a still made from the videotape and brought it over so we could canvass the stores in the area. "Actually, you were pretty damn smart. Oh, I don't mean you're some kind of forensics expert, but you figured keeping the body cold would make it appear that Julie died later, after you were gone. The tricky part must have been knocking her out. What did you do? Grab her by the hair and smash her head back into the faucet?"

"*No*—"

"Oh, come on. It's my word against yours. The police are

closing the file. I just want to know."

"It was an accident," he said thickly.

"Neal—"

"It *was*. I heard her fall—a big splash—and I went in and saw her—" He broke off, remembering.

"And you just stood there and watched her drown. No, wait." I hadn't thought I could feel any more disgust, but I did. "You went out and closed the door and came back when it was over, didn't you?"

Something shifted in his eyes. He shrugged, and the slightest smile hovered on his lips. "Like you said. Your word against mine. Forget the lawsuit. I think I'll keep the videotape of me and Suzanne for a souvenir, and we'll call it square."

"Sure," I said. "You can start a collection."

I gestured to the young Vietnamese fellow who stood way over by the cactus garden, his video camera with its high-powered zoom lens focused on us. Danny gave me a thumbs-up, and I flipped up my shirt collar so Neal could see the remote mike.

"You can't do that," he said.

"Oh, I don't know. I guess a court might find the tape inadmissible, but then again, maybe not. At any rate all the talk shows and those sleazoid news magazines, boy, they'll love it."

He stopped smiling. To tell the truth, for somebody who was about to have his fifteen minutes of fame, the man was downright glum.

Deal with the Devil

Two things I swore I'd never do—go voluntarily east of Phoenix in the winter and do business with the mob. But here I was on a bitterly cold February morning, driving across dreary Kansas plains to the federal prison in Leavenworth to visit Joe "The Pole" Maggiano, shivering and lecturing myself on such things as ethics and moral values as I followed the guard to Maggiano's spartan cell.

The old mafioso greeted me politely. He looked shriveled and defanged but was reputed to have personally killed four men and ordered the death of dozens more.

"So you have come to see the devil," he said in a dry, papery voice. "What finally convinced you?"

"The autopsy pictures of your granddaughter."

He gestured to a framed photo of a dark-haired young woman on his wall. "My beautiful Angelina, before those animals, those gang-bangers got to her." He fixed his rheumy eyes on me. "You have come a long way for a personal visit, Mrs. West. Tell me how I can persuade you to take the job."

"Two things: First, if I find enough hard evidence, the man will be turned over to the police. Second, whatever the outcome, I will never hear from you or any of your people ever again for any reason." And then I named my price.

"Agreed," he said, offered me a bony hand to seal the bargain, and began to speak of Angelina Martin, his daughter's daughter.

I had heard most of this from one of his people, how Angelina lived long enough to say that the man who drove her home from a party had kicked her out of his car when she re-fused to perform oral sex; how she died before identifying him. The young woman's connection to the Family was never publicized. Pressure was brought to bear, Maggiano said, so as not to alert the animals who did the actual killing or the thirty-one men who attended the party. Whacking them all was still an option, but he hoped I could discover which one left Angelina in South Central L.A. that hot July night. No mention of tracking down the gang members; somehow I thought that had been an in-house job, already accom-plished.

When I asked why me, old Joe said, "Sometimes my people are neither subtle nor discreet. I'm told you can be both."

"By whom?"

"Let's just say you were highly recommended."

All the way back to California I tried to figure out who I knew that could be so closely connected to the Mafia and concluded I didn't really want to know.

Six weeks later I'd worked my way down Maggiano's list—discreetly, as advertised—to Nick Willis, a promoter and pro-ducer in the recording industry who had built his career on scamming. One thing about con artists: they are the easiest people in the world to snow. A snap to convince Nick that I was a reporter for *Living in Style* magazine and wanted nothing more than to give him some free ink. When he sug-gested I go with him on a jaunt to New York, it seemed like a good way to do some digging up close and personal.

"Keep your eyes open and your mouth closed, honey," he said as he hustled me off the plane at JFK. Just inside the ter-minal several drivers held signs with the names of their ex-pected passengers. Nick walked briskly to a man waiting for RENFROW and let the driver limo him and me into the city, leaving the real Mr. Renfrow to fend for himself.

This was an omen of things to come. Days, doing business, he was never happy unless somebody got screwed. Nights, I was the target of choice. He tried everything to get me in bed from sly charm and hints of lavish gifts to not-so-veiled threats, including his drunken warning that last night as we taxied through Harlem about what happened to women who weren't nice to him—"like that little wop bitch I once kicked out of the car."

He apologized on the flight back to L.A., although hinting that it was really all my fault, being such a tease, and then made one more proposition as we entered the terminal. Amazing that he never worried about how he'd be portrayed in print; I guess he considered his behavior macho and cute. Picking the nearest driver with a cardboard placard, I said to Nick loudly enough so the driver could hear, "Oh, that's you, isn't it?"

He shrugged, giving up on me and opting for a free ride, saying, "Let me know when you get a pub date," as he hurried the driver away.

If I had really tried, could I have dug up enough solid evidence to convict Nick Willis? Maybe, but probably not. My word against his. Too late anyway, because I'd kept my deal with the devil, made a call from a payphone before the flight left New York, and handed Nick off to the fellow in LAX whose sign read: MAGGIANO.

I'll say one thing about the mob. They settle their accounts promptly. Within the week I had a check drawn on a properly laundered corporate account for my expenses plus a copy of the letter that accompanied the donation to a home for battered women—one million dollars made in Angelina Martin's name.

Diamonds Are for Never

I had never been a diamond courier before, and by the time I got back to L.A. I'd decided I never would be again. There are too many people in this world who wouldn't think twice about hacking off a hand so they could take the briefcase manacled to a person's wrist, like about half the passengers milling around at Kennedy in New York as well as several on my plane. I even had my suspicions about the flight attendant who seemed overly attentive, constantly stopping by with coffee refills.

But then, of course, I have an overactive imagination. It comes with the PI territory. And I'd had a very long day, trying to get in and out of New York City before what would hereafter be referred to as the "Snowstorm of the Century" came blasting in. I'd even given up the convenience of flying from Orange County's John Wayne Airport and made the fifty-mile drive north to Los Angeles International so I could get direct flights and make my round trip in less than twenty-four hours.

At 9 p.m. my big DC-10 glided down over the bright sweep of the L.A. basin, right on schedule. Since I had no luggage, I managed to make a quick exit, draping my jacket over my arm to hide the manacles and hoping I looked like any other harried businesswoman as I plowed through the crowds around the Jetway.

My assistant, Danny Thu, was supposed to be waiting out in the parking structure across from Terminal Four. I dug my cell phone from my purse and called him on the run. He answered on the second ring.

"On my way out," I said.

"Right," Danny said. "Uh, Delilah? There's been a slight change. Mr. Boudreau is with me. We're going up to Santa Monica from here."

I groaned at the prospect of my long day dragging on indefinitely and muttered, "Oh, great."

Well, that's not an exact quote. My words were a tad more colorful and delivered in a loud enough voice to earn me an approving grin from a skinny, denim-clad, pasty-faced Gen-Xer with a backpack slung over one shoulder. Male, I guessed—he looked like he posed for heroin-chic ads in *Vanity Fair* and *Cosmo*.

I vowed on the spot to clean up my language.

I also ended my call and walked faster to be sure I arrived at the curb outside baggage claim before Danny got chased off by some overly efficient cop. There was a million dollars worth of diamonds in the briefcase. That was wholesale value. Lord knows what the markup to retail would be. I didn't particularly relish the idea of hanging out curbside looking out for thieves with oversized pruning shears while Danny was forced to circle the huge U-shaped airport.

Just before we landed, the pilot had announced that it was 49 degrees at LAX. This was not exactly warm for Southern California, but as I stepped outside the terminal it felt downright balmy compared to the icy blasts of wind that had skirted down New York's concrete canyons. Even an outlander like me could smell the promise of wet, heavy snow, and I was more than happy to be back here inhaling that distinct L.A. odor of ozone and exhaust.

I spotted my blue Astrovan right away, double-parked with Danny at the wheel. Headlights from a continuous stream of cars, shuttle vans, and buses made up for the dim illumination. I could see Leo Boudreau's blocky silhouette just behind Danny.

I jumped into the passenger seat, slammed the door, and felt vast relief because basically my job was over. I was about to deliver the diamonds to my client, even if he happened to be sitting in my vehicle rather than waiting for me in his jewelry store in Newport Beach as planned.

"Any problems?" Boudreau asked.

I might have mentioned too little sleep, close encounters with New York cab drivers, and eleven hours of airline seats and airline food, not to mention my preoccupation with the prospect of being rudely detached from the briefcase.

Determined not to sound like a wuss, I shook my head and said, "Just the weather," while I fished a key from my purse, unlocked the manacles, and passed the briefcase back to him.

"You got out just in time," Danny said. "I heard on the radio that they closed Kennedy, must have been about two hours after you left."

Danny was already rolling. He left the inner lanes, swung out around a cab divider, and plunged into the dodge-ball traffic with the confidence of somebody whose main mode of transportation is a bicycle. He rides to UCI where he's completing a double major in business and computer science, through rush-hour traffic on the days he works in my office, and in biking marathons on weekends. This keeps my young assistant whip-thin and full of crackling energy. It also makes him absolutely fearless behind a wheel.

He flashed me a grin as I quickly fastened my seat belt.

Boudreau said impatiently, "Could I have some light back here?"

I had to undo the seat belt for a second so I could reach up and turn on the overhead light. Buckled back in, I turned to watch Boudreau unlock the briefcase.

53

He was in his late forties, good-looking in an overbearing sort of way, vain enough to keep his big hands carefully manicured and to be wearing a suit and a tie when something more casual would have done just as well. I wasn't quite sure all that thick, dark hair really belonged to him, but then, as we know, I have a suspicious mind.

"I assume we're going to the Gemological Institute," I said. "That wasn't part of the deal."

"I told you I wanted Moira to inspect the diamonds as soon as you arrived," he said testily. "I don't appreciate having to go all the way to Santa Monica either, but something came up. She's stuck at the lab."

So why not stash the diamonds in his safe at the store until his expert could come take a look? I didn't even bother to ask. If you didn't know the guy, you'd think his square-shouldered, square-jawed look suggested forthrightness. I'd quickly learned it just meant he was incredibly pigheaded.

Of course, his insistence on an immediate inspection suggested that he was more suspicious of me than of the diamond merchants back in New York. This bugged me, but, hey, if I had a cool million on the line, I'd be paranoid, too.

Inside the briefcase was a specially fitted insert, sectioned into little boxes and velvet-lined, covered by a plastic lid. Each cut, polished diamond was in its own tiny plastic Baggie labeled with a lot number. Then the diamonds appeared to be sorted by approximate weight, maybe seventy-five stones, most of them at least a carat.

In New York I'd had to wait while each stone was checked off an inventory sheet, thinking all the while that only a carefully controlled supply by a certain South African cartel made the sparkling rocks so valuable.

From the beginning I'd had my doubts about the courier bit. Myself, I think I would've put the gems in a sock and stuck them down in some dirty clothes in a carry-on. When I asked the wholesaler about the way they normally shipped diamonds, I was told the usual method was parcel post and not even insured. Boudreau was about the only retailer who wanted personal delivery. This last information was said politely enough but in such a way that there was no doubt Boudreau was considered a fool for this idiosyncrasy.

Now, behind me Boudreau took a long look to verify that I had indeed brought gemstones instead of some New York red-hots, his inspection taking much too long to suit my frayed nerves. I cast an anxious glance around at the bumper-to-bumper traffic on Century Boulevard. The side windows of the van were tinted. I doubted anybody could see in. Still, I felt better when Boudreau closed up the briefcase.

And a whole lot better when Danny murmured, "Glove box is unlocked," and I knew that if I had to I could get to the .38 I keep there.

Traffic was heavy but moving as we headed north on the 405. Boudreau wasn't much for small talk, thank goodness, because fatigue was fast catching up with me, and what energy I had left was spent on making sure nobody was tailing us. He sat with the case on his knees for the thirty-minute trip, silent except to give Danny directions on where to exit and how to find the institute.

The place didn't look like much from the outside, just a big nondescript building that could just as easily have housed a Wal-Mart. All the spaces out front said *reserved*. Probably not enforced this time of night but Danny said he'd wait in the van.

Boudreau carried the briefcase and rang a buzzer next to a door where the glass revealed an inner barrier of steel bars. A polite male voice over an intercom requested our names; then there was some silence while we got checked out. Waiting, I noticed a surveillance camera and a decal warning that security was provided by one of the best companies in the business. After a couple of minutes an armed guard came to let us in, a burly guy with a side arm only slightly smaller than a cannon. He was accompanied by a woman Boudreau introduced as Moira Sweeney.

After a distracted nod returned the guard to his post, Moira said, "Come on back to the lab."

She was shorter than my five-seven, one of those thin, fox-faced women that look as though they are being consumed by some inner fire. Her kinky red hair was brittle and dry, and her pale, freckled skin had unhealthy sallow undertones and looked stretched over the bones of her nose and cheeks.

She walked quickly, leading the way down a hall through a rabbit warren of darkened rooms with numbers on closed doors that gave no hint of their purposes. Boudreau was a step behind, grousing about having to come up from Orange County.

"I told you, Leo, it got hectic," Moira said, sounding edgy and stressed. "A large stone," she explained for my benefit as she stopped to unlock a door marked simply LAB. "Our policy is to process and return it the same day. Come on in."

Overhead lights were on in the bunker-like room, and one of the big microscopes on the long bench was lit. There were maybe twenty microscopes in all, each with a high stool in front of it. Shelving beneath the bench was sectioned into cubbyholes, many of these spaces crowded with an assortment of binders and metal and plastic containers. Beside Moira's scope some kind of logbook lay open.

There was a faint, oily smell in the room, but that was being quickly overpowered by the aroma of coffee brewing in a machine down on the end of the lab bench.

"I'm just finishing up here," Moira said. "Leo, why don't

you and Ms. West help yourselves to a cup of coffee, give me a minute, and then I'll get to your stones."

She reached for the briefcase. This was Boudreau's expert and one we'd gone out of our way to see, but he hesitated for a second before he yielded the case.

I had assumed their relationship to be business, but now I was picking up on the kind of subtle tension that suggested more. He stood a little too close, invading her space. And there was a kind of tug of war going on, some sort of power thing. And maybe a flicker of triumph in her eyes as she took the case and put it on the bench.

Something else I noticed: Moira wasn't dressed the way a woman does for a lover. She wore a white blouse tucked into plain khaki slacks, an old, shapeless green cardigan, and some scuffed black leather flats. She hadn't bothered to put on any lipstick or powder her nose.

Well, maybe their intimacy was a thing of the past, but I'd bet there had been some. *And none of your business,* I told myself as I headed back to the coffee machine.

I kept glancing back at Moira, and so did Boudreau. She wrote something in the logbook, closed it, and shoved it into the cubbyhole beneath the bench. Then she opened the briefcase containing the diamonds and snapped up the lid that covered the inner compartment.

I poured coffee into two of those waxed paper cups with the foldout, pinch-together handles and handed one to Boudreau. There was a bowl with a sign that said, *twenty-five cents, please,* but he ignored it. He only took time to dump some sweetener into his cup, then went back to join Moira.

I threw in a couple of quarters, figuring it was worth it just to hear him holler when I put the contribution on my expense account.

57

Yeah, I admit it. I was not particularly fond of Leo Boudreau.

Meanwhile, Moira had taken out the inventory list, Boudreau quickly gulped his coffee, and the two began careful count of the stones, Moira reading the lot number from the little plastic Baggies and Boudreau checking off each one.

I wondered if anybody would object to my moving one of the other stools over. Decided, what the hell, I didn't need to peer over their shoulders. I yawned and wished for a big comfortable couch, or at least a back to the stool next to Moira's where I sat, leaning against the hard edge of the counter, drinking the hot, strong coffee, and wondering why he needed a gemologist to check an inventory list.

Then, the count completed, Moira took a headpiece from the bench and put it on. The contraption had an eye loupe and a big square light-housing that stuck out beyond that, very bright light when she switched it on. She opened one of the Baggies, removed a diamond with a pair of oversize tweezers, held the stone in front of the loupe, and turned back and forth for what seemed like a hell of a long time.

"What?" Boudreau said, reading something in her face, then hoarsely, "Jesus, is it—?"

"See for yourself." Moira took off the headpiece and gave it to him. Held the stone in front of the eye loupe so he could verify what she'd seen.

He pretty quickly ripped off the headpiece and handed it back, looking as though the coffee he'd drunk a few minutes earlier was on its way back up. I put my cup down carefully, knowing just how he felt.

"Fake?" I asked.

"Oh, it's real enough," Moira said. "Real cubic zirconia."

By the time Moira got through enough of the stones to

figure they were all fakes, Boudreau was holding on to the bench, looking almost as green as her sweater. Good thing I was sitting down. My knees probably would have folded up on me. Just the velocity of the thoughts spinning in my head could have sent me falling on my face.

The stones had been placed in the inner compartment of the briefcase right in front of me in the diamond mart back in New York. The case had been closed and handcuffed to my wrist. I hadn't unlocked the manacles until I was in the van with Boudreau. I hadn't even unlocked the damn things when I used the lavatory on the airplane. Talk about awkward.

I had insisted that Boudreau buy the seat next to me on the flight to L.A., so it would remain empty. I had avoided conversations with strangers. Had drunk no alcohol. Had not fallen asleep—well, maybe I'd nodded off a couple of times, but never long enough for somebody to search me for the keys, unlock the cuffs, open the case, and substitute phonies for the real diamonds.

Assuming they were genuine to begin with. Could the switch have taken place back in New York? Would an old, established firm really do something like that?

I knew Boudreau would never believe it. There was only one person he would hold responsible for the theft.

"You—" He wheeled around, teeth bared and ready to go for my throat. "What the bloody hell have you done with my diamonds?"

It turns out this was not a rhetorical question. As far as he was concerned, I was a thief, no question about it. He wouldn't for one second entertain the idea that the switch took place in New York, and it certainly couldn't have happened after I climbed into the van with him and Danny. That left the time in-between, with me as the only culprit.

"Just a damn minute," I said, breaking into his tirade. "If you really think I stole your diamonds, call the police. Make a formal complaint. But you'd better be sure you want to do that because when we find out what really happened, I'll sue your ass for defamation of character."

Not that I could really afford a lawsuit. Not that I was ready to risk wrangling with some cops who might look at the situation just the way Boudreau did. But I was mad, and my bluster seemed to make him hesitate.

"Leo, think," Moira said. "Are you sure you want the police in on this right now? I know you'll need to file a report for insurance purposes, but can't it wait? I can put the case in the safe until morning. We'll all have clearer heads then."

"And give her time to leave the country?" Boudreau shot me another glare, but I could see the wheels turning, some kind of frantic calculation going on.

Uncertain just how much ID the diamond wholesaler would require, I had taken my passport along to New York. Now I took it from my purse and handed it to Moira.

"Lock that up with the case," I said, adding to Boudreau, "For your information, the only place I'm going is home to bed." I was tempted to add that he could damn well find his own way south to Orange County, but I knew it wasn't smart to make him even madder. "If you want a lift, let's go."

"Moira can take me."

"You have to be kidding." There was enough ice in her voice to tell me she didn't expect to be asked to stay the night and she wasn't about to make a three-hour round-trip drive for him.

He didn't like it, but in the end, after the briefcase was locked in the lab safe along with my passport, we agreed to meet Moira back at the institute at ten o'clock the following morning, and Boudreau made the grim journey home with Danny and me.

To Danny's questioning look, I muttered, "Don't ask," and waited until we dropped off Boudreau at his store before I explained.

Looking as sick as I felt, Danny said, "I couldn't tell you earlier, but there's something else you ought to know. Boudreau's check—your retainer? It bounced."

Even though I was exhausted, I woke up before dawn and tossed and turned for a while, my anger growing by the minute. Bad enough to be accused of being a thief. Downright insulting to get stiffed out of my fee as well.

A shower and a jolt of caffeine cleared my head enough so I could do some thinking, and what I thought was that of the three people in that lab the night before, I was the only one who didn't know squat about diamonds.

Moira had said the stones were fake, Boudreau had agreed, and I had accepted what they said. But assume that everything that had occurred up to that point happened just the way I thought it had: I'd picked up real diamonds from a reliable dealer in New York and delivered them without incident to Boudreau in California. That being so, I could draw only one conclusion: The diamonds that Moira and Boudreau inspected had been the genuine articles.

Assuming *that,* then what did we have?

Insurance fraud was the first thing that came to mind. The two of them working the scam together was the second, quickly followed by the third, which was that exhaustion the night before was no excuse. It had been the worst kind of stupidity to let Moira keep the briefcase. If the diamonds had not been phonies when I delivered them, they surely would be by now.

Bloody hell, I thought and figured I might as well go stomp around my office rather than my apartment.

I went to join the rest of the crowd on the road in the chilly darkness with the fond hope of beating the rush hour. No big jams yet, but plenty of small ones and time to try and figure out what Moira and Boudreau would do next and to wonder at what point I should call a lawyer.

At the office, I found Danny's bike chained to a post in the parking lot and Danny upstairs in front of the computer.

"Couldn't sleep," Danny said. "I thought it wouldn't hurt to have some background on Boudreau."

What he had was pretty complete. Most of it had been obtained through perfectly legal research. As for the rest—I didn't want to know.

Scanning the reports, I saw that Boudreau had divorced his wife the year before and remarried. He lived in a pricey condo near Fashion Island, leased a Lexus and a Beemer, had been in the jewelry business for fifteen years. That was on the surface. Dig a little deeper and you found that, like a lot of people these days, the guy was skimming along on the edge of financial disaster: the condo mortgaged to the hilt, behind on child support for the two kids by his first wife, credit cards maxed out, his business close to going down the tubes, and checks bouncing all over the place. It was clear he didn't have the million to pay for the diamond shipment. He had a loan lined up, however, some bank ready to take a chance as long as there was collateral.

If the insurance company paid off on the diamonds, then he and Moira sold the stones, how much money would he wind up with? Not a fortune, but in his situation any infusion of cash would be a blessing.

It was a logical explanation, but I would have felt a lot better about buying into it completely if a couple of things hadn't been nagging at me. One was the look on Leo Boudreau's face when I mentioned calling the cops, even though he would have to make the report before he could file a claim. The other was the mention of all those rubber checks.

I remembered Boudreau's insurance carrier, the name having been on one of the forms I'd handed over in New York. I called them from the van while crawling through some serious rush-hour traffic on the way to Santa Monica.

A little bit of tap dancing and a few outright lies got me the information that threw my insurance fraud theory out the window. There was no coverage on the diamonds. The check for the premium, like my retainer, had bounced.

Leo Boudreau was already at the institute when I arrived, some ten minutes late. He was in the entry area arguing with a slender, tweedy man whose plastic nametag read *C. Goodykamp, Ph.D.*

Mostly Boudreau was doing the arguing, or rather the bellowing. The soft-spoken Dr. Goodykamp was holding his own, however, even though Boudreau kept cutting him off in mid-sentence.

"This is ridiculous," Boudreau said. "Moira wouldn't just take off."

"Mr. Boudreau, you're not listening," Dr. Goodykamp began. "She—"

"We had an appointment, dammit," Boudreau yelled. "Tell him, Delilah. Ten o'clock. We were meeting her here."

"That was the plan," I said. Since it was obvious Boudreau wasn't going to, I introduced myself and asked, "Where is she?"

"On vacation," Dr. Goodykamp said.

"She can't be," Boudreau said.

"Well, she is. She called first thing this morning and asked me to give you the briefcase you left here. If you'll excuse me, I'll go get it from the safe."

He hurried off, and I turned to Boudreau. "I think I owe you an apology. Guess you weren't in on it after all."

"What are you talking about?"

"Face it, Leo," I said. "Moira Sweeney stole your diamonds."

"No way." He glared at me, but the look on his face told me he was resisting an unwelcome reality check. "You don't understand. We were—close, for a while. *Intimate*."

Surprise, surprise.

"I know Moira," he went on. "For one thing, she wouldn't have the guts to do something like this. And even if she did, when could she have done it? There was no time to switch the stones."

I don't know which bothered him more, the fact that Moira would actually have the chutzpah to take such a chance or the possibility that he had been taken in by her guile.

"I think she did it while we were getting the coffee," I said. "And she didn't have to switch them all. How many did you look at? One? She knew you trusted her, figured after you saw a sample or two you'd take her word on the rest. If you didn't, well, you'd think somebody skimmed a couple of stones instead of stealing the whole lot."

"Jesus," he said, panic replacing his disbelief. "You have to find her before she sells my diamonds, before she leaves the country."

"I'd be happy to, but there's one little problem. I don't work without a retainer. Of course, you're so tapped out, you can't even cover my courier charges, so how about I take a finder's fee. Ten percent, that should do it."

"What?" His face seemed to swell up, and it turned a dull red. "I'm not paying you anything. You find her, or I'll call the police. I'll tell them you did it, that you and Moira were in it together."

"Go ahead," I said. "By the time the cops get up to speed, Moira could be in Rio. And here you'd be. No insurance, and you'll still owe your wholesalers back in New York. And think of all the free publicity I'm going to make sure you get. Bet the tabloids love it."

"You really are a heartless bitch," he said bitterly.

"Damn straight," I said. "Do we have a deal or not?"

Boudreau agreed to my terms, but he was not happy about it. I figured he was already hatching up a plan to make sure I didn't see even a *one*-percent recovery fee, let alone ten.

Except for a current address, he could supply little information about Moira's private life, which didn't surprise me much. I decided to start at the institute and hoped to find somebody who could provide a lead to Moira's whereabouts.

Covering all the bases, I suggested that we have another gemologist inspect the contents of the briefcase, and for once Boudreau didn't put up an argument. When Dr. Goodykamp returned with the case, I explained what was going on. He looked shaken by the news, but not exactly overwhelmed by disbelief, even when we opened the briefcase and found that it was empty.

After I convinced Boudreau to go back to Orange County, not the easiest job, I asked Goodykamp if we could find someplace to talk, alone.

"My office," he said without much enthusiasm.

We entered a small cubicle, sparsely furnished. A Shaker desk held nothing except a telephone and a note pad with a pen lined up beside it. These two items were placed squarely in front of a black leather chair. Most of a bookcase was used to display chunks of amethyst crystal, geodes sliced in half to reveal their intricate structure, polished slabs of petrified wood.

There was one straight-backed chair against the wall. Without waiting for an invitation, I picked it up, planted it in front of the desk, and sat down. Goodykamp sighed as he took a seat across from me.

I said, "When Moira called this morning, you're sure she didn't tell you where she was going?"

"This morning?" He considered briefly and seemed happy to say, "No. She didn't mention it."

"How long have you known Moira?"

"Several years. Since she came to work here."

What can I say? Sometimes you get lucky.

"You're friends?" I asked, sure of the answer.

"Friends, yes. We certainly are." He frowned down at the notepad, moved it a fraction of an inch to the left, a hair toward me.

"She's in serious trouble," I said.

"Yes, I know. But I can't help you, Ms. West. So please don't ask."

"You have it wrong," I said. "You'd be helping *her* by telling me where she is. Let me talk to her and take a shot at persuading her to give back the diamonds before Boudreau goes to the cops."

"He would, too," Goodykamp said. "Moira keeps things to herself, but she's told me enough so I know what a rotten man he is." He paused, clearly torn. "I'm really worried about her, Ms. West. She's let her health go downhill. She can't be thinking straight to do something this bizarre, this desperate."

"Then, please," I said. "Where is she?"

"At my place." Relief was mixed with the guilt in the admission. "I'll give you the address."

Goodykamp's small home was in an older section of Santa Monica in what the social engineers like to say is a neighborhood in transition. This meant the houses had been mostly turned into run-down rentals where stucco was crumbling, paint was peeling, and weeds and crabgrass were taking back the yards.

Under a gray marine overcast, the area had a sad, hunkered-down look—although, come to think of it, I wasn't sure that sunshine would help much.

A fairly new Saturn sat in the driveway, and smoke curled from a chimney, so Dr. Goodykamp must have kept his promise not to call. Still, when Moira opened the door, she didn't seem all that surprised to see me. She leaned against the doorjamb, looking pale, gaunt, and exhausted, wearing the same clothes she'd worn the night before.

"Poor Goody," she said. "I put him in such a spot asking to stay here last night. I hope he's not too upset."

"He's worried about you. We need to talk, Moira."

"Okay." She stood aside to let me in. "He didn't know about the diamonds. Please remember that."

Down here near the coast, there was a distinct chill in the air, cool enough to make the blazer I wore over my slacks feel good. The temperature was nothing like the bone-deep cold of that wind back in New York, nothing that warranted the bonfire that roared in the living room fireplace.

The place was so warm I immediately took off my jacket. I could feel the heat on my face and hung back, but Moira went to sit right in front of the fire on an old armchair. In contrast to his office, Dr. Goodykamp's home was comfortably cluttered, and I'd bet on a few dust bunnies over in the corners.

"Did Leo turn me in?" Moira asked.

"Not yet. There's still time to straighten this out."

"Time? No, you're wrong about that." She hugged herself, wrapping the green sweater tightly around her body. "Do you know how long I let Leo jerk me around? Ten years."

"We all do dumb things," I said. Sweat popped out along my hairline, but I was willing to sit on the couch as far from the fire as possible, drip a little perspiration, and listen to her story if it meant getting her to give up the diamonds.

"Well, I was dumber than most," she said. "He kept promising to divorce his wife, and I believed him until I just couldn't swallow his lies anymore. I was taking some courses at the institute while I worked at his store. When they offered me a job, I grabbed it. I thought I could break away from Leo, but I didn't, of course. He could always talk me into anything, like being his courier, back and forth to New York. I did that for a long time, even though I hated it." She stared into the fire where fierce blue flames consumed two huge hunks of oak that lay atop a bed of glowing embers. "When Leo got his divorce, he didn't say a word about it. A friend down in Orange County saw an announcement in the newspaper when he got married again."

"So you decided to pay him back," I said. "I can understand that, believe me. But this is not the way, Moira. Walk away from him. Have a good life. That would be the best revenge."

She gave me a bleak smile, wintry in that tropical room. "We all think like that, don't we? We think we have forever. I did. Then, three weeks ago I found out I have pancreatic cancer."

"Ah, God," I said sadly, knowing as soon as she said it, she was telling the truth.

Moira said, "So you see, the time Leo stole from me is a lot more precious than it would be for most people."

"Yes, it would be."

I might have added how sorry I was for her, but the words seemed too trite, too knee-jerk to offer.

"So you planned to do what?" I asked. "Sell the diamonds to pay hospital bills? Leave the money to your family? To charity?"

"No, nothing like that. Nothing so noble." She gave me the ghost of a smile. "Did you ever see that James Bond movie where they hide the diamonds in a corpse, and recover them after the corpse is cremated? Pure Hollywood, Delilah. It could never happen. Because diamonds are carbon. Pure, and beautiful, but carbon all the same. Given a hot enough fire . . ."

"*Jesus,*" I whispered, following her gaze to the fireplace and understanding only then the depth of her hatred for Leo Boudreau.

"You might as well call the police," she said.

I was too stunned to say anything for a few seconds, but then I asked, "What were your plans before I showed up?"

"I was going to stay here and make sure Goody's house didn't burn down," she said. "Then I thought I'd head south, go to the Baja. I know a place. It's cheap. There's a clinic. I don't think they're such sticklers about pain medication in Mexico. I wrote a couple of letters," she added. "Mailed them this morning. One to Leo, explaining just how badly I've screwed up his life. One to Goody to pass on to the police so they'd know you were not involved."

What the hell, I thought. What would I have done with ten percent of a million bucks anyway?

I said, "If you get going, you might make it through L.A. before the rush hour."

She left quickly, pausing only to say thanks and give me a quick hug. After she was gone, I opened a few windows to cool off the place, and then I called Boudreau. I told him I'd tracked her down, but, gee, wouldn't you know, she had already flown the coop. And all the while I thought about him reading that letter from Moira while I watched the oak logs in the fireplace turn to ashes and those million-dollar embers disintegrate in an eerie blue-white glow.

Somewhere South of Melrose

My work as a private detective tends to send me off in all directions from my home base down in Orange County, but it had been a while since anything had brought me to Tinsel Town. Now I was here because of where I'd grown up and the people I'd known back then, cruising slowly down Hollywood Boulevard past Vine and wondering when the place had started to look like a foreign country.

I had a sudden vivid memory of being jammed into an old convertible, of a giddiness compounded of youth and beer bought with phony ID, of crowding into theaters that were still the place to be for first-run shows and sightings of movie stars, as well as some lusty teenage groping. Today the Chinese was one of the few still open and doing business. The Hollywood Theater was now a Guinness Museum, and the Vogue had become a center for paranormal research.

Never mind the nice new buildings scattered among the old, compliments of the riots a few years back. Even in a wash of glorious noon-high sunlight there was still a seedier, sadder air. Maybe it was the preponderance of fast food joints, tattoo parlors and body-piercing shops, or the fact that the tourists gawking at the inlaid stars on the sidewalks were outnumbered by hookers and drifters.

Or maybe I'd just edited the memories, letting years of movies and TV shows add a golden, glamorous skim. In any case I was already regretting the nostalgic impulse that had sent me blocks north of my destination. I turned on a cross street and headed South.

Past Melrose things got worse. No seedy glitter here. Just plenty of graffiti, dirt and hopelessness as I located the address and found a place to squeeze the van in along the curb.

I counted a good dozen homeless people who sat in the lip of shadow cast by the old three-story building, where most of the downstairs windows had boards instead of glass. One lone bag lady shuffled along the street, pushing a shopping cart. A cluster of homeboys eyed me from their station by a bus stop bench.

A holster clipped to the back waistband of my slacks holds my mini-automatic. I took my .38 from the glove box and let it keep the Beretta company. The artillery made me feel only slightly better, but since chances were good that I'd come back to find a window in the van smashed and the interior looted at least I could take some comfort in knowing that the revolver wouldn't be stolen and used in a drive-by.

I climbed out of the van, already having second thoughts. This might be Crystal Landry's last known address, but she'd lived here more than twenty years ago. I'd bet that even in its heyday the apartment-hotel was a place for transients where no questions were asked or forwarding addresses given. So what were the chances Crystal was around, or that anybody here remembered her?

Nil to zero.

Still, since the guilds had no record of Crystal, and I'd struck out at the library for the Academy of Motion Picture Arts and Sciences, this was all I had left.

As I locked the van, the homeboys began to drift my way. They wore no common colors, so I guessed they were just your average, nonaffiliated gang-bangers. Somehow this did not make me feel more secure. Sunlight glinted off an earring, a nose stud, a length of shiny bicycle chain pulled through one fellow's belt loops.

Oh, yeah, I was in a foreign land, all right, and the natives were restless.

If anybody asked I'd tell them I grew up in L.A., which to most people means Hollywood, and I did. Well, I lived a few freeway miles east in Altadena, close enough. That's where I had I gone to high school with Crystal Landry—and with Alan Weems who was now my client.

Alan had tracked me down, using, of all things, one of those chatty letters from one of our ex-classmates, trying to tempt us into coming for a reunion. You know the kind of letter, lots of rah-rah and hyped-up success stories about the alumni designed to make the rest of us want to come and bask in reflected glory. This one included me on the roster of interesting grads. While I missed most successful and most prolific child bearer, I did get a mention for most unusual occupation, including a description of work that somehow made me sound like a cross between Miss Marple and one of the sleazier sex kittens from a James Bond movie.

When the letter was followed by a phone call from a member of the reunion committee, grown desperate enough to beat the bushes, I begged off, saying I was packing my knitted shawl and stiletto-heeled boots and flying off that weekend to South America to seduce the head of the Colombia drug cartel. Sitting across my desk from me in my Santa Ana office after the reunion was long past, Alan confessed that he had attended, the first time he'd ever been to one of the shindigs, and then only in the hope of seeing Crystal.

"She didn't come," Alan said. "I found out she wasn't even on the mailing list."

Men change a lot after their teens, I had discovered, a lot more than women, and he looked only vaguely like the boy

I'd gone to school with. The long-limbed grace was hidden behind some extra pounds and an improperly tailored suit, the track-star confidence chipped away by continuing doses of reality that life keeps handing out. His thick, sun-streaked hair had thinned and darkened. His clear blue eyes had crow's-feet at the corners and watched the world with caution.

"I couldn't believe how disappointed I was," he went on. "How I'd built it up in my mind. And afterward, well, I just couldn't stop thinking about her. God, Delilah, we were so crazy about each other."

"Oh, yeah," I said.

I'd never been included in their inner circle, but I certainly remembered the supercharged glow that seemed to radiate when the two came together.

They were the perfect couple, above all the teenage angst, destined for happy-ever-after. A little envy there, I admit it. I'd spent my high school days walking a fine line between adolescent rebellion and keeping my nose clean. Or at least clean enough so nothing got back to my tough-minded dad who had spent enough years on the L.A.P.D. to have little patience with minor acts of anarchy.

Trying not to sound too wistful, I said, "I figured you and Crystal for a sure thing."

"Yeah," Alan said. "Me, too."

But when he left for Berkeley that fall, Crystal went off to look for the real Hollywood in Burbank and Culver City. And it was scary how quickly she vanished, Alan said. Her phone was disconnected just before Thanksgiving. By Christmas there was nobody at her last address who remembered her. And the aunt who had raised Crystal after her parents died had moved away, leaving no forwarding address.

Crystal might have been a star in all those high school productions of *West Side Story* and *A Midsummer Night's Dream*, but I'd bet her luminous beauty dimmed considerably next to the megawatt competition, and none of those big fantasy-factory doors ever opened. At any rate, I'd never spotted her on the screen, big or small. Alan said he hadn't, either.

"For a long time I kept looking," he said, "but I guess it didn't happen for her."

Meanwhile, Alan's heart mended, after a fashion. He met somebody else, fell in love and got married. The childless marriage ended in divorce a few months before the reunion. Which explained why Alan became obsessed with thoughts of what might have been.

Psychologists testify to the power of that first deep love, how the remarkable pull of it continues to alter our lives. I know about this firsthand because I'm the person who gets to look at the old pictures and listen to the longings that never seem to go away.

So these folks come to me, and more often than not I find their lost love. What's amazing is how in a lot of cases passion does rebloom. Sometimes, once in a while, there are even happy endings.

Not always, however.

Too bad I didn't remember that before I went to look for Crystal.

"Pick your battles," my dad had told me the day I graduated from the police academy. "Don't die stupid."

I always try to heed my father's advice, even though it means I have to overcome my natural tendency to dig in my heels and stand my ground. Besides, I wasn't getting paid for this kind of duty. So I had already backtracked a couple of steps toward the van when a lowrider Cutlass came barreling up and spared me the embarrassment of a full retreat.

The homeboys piled in, off to more important targets, saying goodbye with catcalls and obscene gestures that crossed all language barriers.

I picked my way through the litter outside the hotel and tried not to breathe too deeply. A little harder to ignore the eyes that watched me. Impossible to shrug off the sense of hopelessness that was as palpable as the smells.

If the building had ever had air-conditioning, it no longer worked. Inside, the floor was sticky under my feet, the air thick with trapped heat and the odors of cigarette smoke, greasy food and despair. I took some comfort from the fact that some twenty-plus years had passed since Crystal had lived here. Surely it couldn't have been this bad a place back then.

The first door on the right had a grimy plaque that read Manager. A knock brought a prolonged fumbling with several dead bolts, accompanied by a litany of curses, and finally a woman squinting through a crack in the door. I got an impression of frizzy red hair, over-baked skin and rampant paranoia honestly earned, in my opinion, by living here.

Neither my state ID nor my declarations of trustworthiness cut any ice with her. But when in doubt, keep talking. I did, and suddenly said the magic word.

"*Crystal?*" she said. "Good God, Crystal *Landry?*"

"You knew her?"

"*Knew* her? We were roommates," she said, opening the door.

What can I say? Sometimes you get lucky.

Inside the one-room studio apartment a floor fan ground away, but did little to cool the stifling air. The weak breeze didn't even ruffle the pages of tabloids and soap opera digests heaped on a coffee table in untidy stacks. Pillows in shades of fuchsia and pink and a few brightly colored Mexican throws faded to hide the murky browns of threadbare carpet and a sagging couch. About the only thing that would have helped this place was a major earthquake with an epicenter at Sunset and Vine.

Shafts of early-afternoon sunshine beamed through boards that covered the window, reflecting off a gallery of framed pictures on the walls. A few were in color, but mostly they were black and white, the kind of publicity photos that arrive on a casting director's desk by the truckload. All of them were of the same young woman, marginally beautiful with a cloud of auburn hair. It took a moment to realize the woman in the photographs was my hostess.

She said her name was Heather Blake. "Well, my *stage* name," she amended, closing the door behind us and engaging all the bolts. "Who did you say you were again?"

"Delilah West."

She shook her mass of over-permed hair, unable to place me, so obviously my fame had not spread north of the Orange County line.

"Kathleen Turner played a private eye," she said. "Some Polish name. Never heard of her, either."

Beyond slender, Heather was bone thin, a gauntness that made me think of eating disorders or the possibility that the long sleeves of her electric blue caftan might hide needle tracks. Right now cheap rum was her drug of choice, mixed with Slim Price cola. There were bottles on a counter in a small kitchenette, and she had a few ounces left in a chunky amber glass.

"Want one?" she offered.

"No, thanks," I said. "Can we sit down and talk about Crystal?"

"Sure. Why not?"

She took one end of the couch. I took the other. It was as uncomfortable as it looked, and the pillows didn't help. Sweat oiled my face, and I was thinking that claustrophobia was a real possibility if I had to live in this cramped, closed-in place.

"You said you were roommates," I prompted.

"Yeah, we were. Right here. Well, upstairs. At first we had singles, but once we got to know each other, it made sense to share. Of course, that ended pretty soon after Carl arrived."

"Carl?"

"Carl—what was it?" She sipped her drink and tried to remember. "Dal—something. Dalpert, I think. God, I still can't believe it. I mean Crystal could've gone somewhere, you know? I mean, look at me. I've been in over a hundred movies and *gobs* of TV shows. I got my AFTRA card. I've worked with Sly and Sharon and Tom, *every*body. I'm reading for a part on 'BayWatch' next week."

"Back up," I said. "You're saying that Crystal gave up on acting?"

"Worse than that," Heather declared, adding with equal amounts of scorn and disbelief, "she went off with Carl to *Fresno*. And she *stayed*. I think she must've *married* the guy."

It took another rum and coke and a pint or two of sweat but I got a fairly good summary of Crystal's brief stopover in Hollywood. She and Heather had plastered the town with head shots, got a couple of gigs together as extras, and had gone to some parties. Between the lines I read of Crystal's plunge into the sleazy swarm of wanna-bes and hangers-on attracted to the sweet promise of fame and fortune like flies to honey.

It was hard to believe she had forgotten Alan so quickly

and fallen for somebody new, but maybe she bought the romantic movie myths and saw Carl as a white knight come to her rescue. This was not Heather's opinion, however.

"Guy was so off," Heather said. "I kept going, *Crys,* what are you thinking? But she wouldn't listen to me."

"What do you mean, off?" I asked.

"You know, a little weird, like he knew something he wasn't telling."

Turns out Carl hadn't revealed much of anything, at least not to Heather. She thought he was a few years older than Crystal. Although he didn't have any visible means of support, he had a red Mustang and enough money to party.

"Was he trying to get into the film business?" I asked.

"Carl? No way," she said. "I don't know *what* that guy was into. I got up one morning, and they were gone. Here I thought Crys and me were friends, and she didn't even say goodbye."

"She was going steady with somebody from high school," I said. "She never even sent a Dear John letter. He came here looking for her at Christmas, but nobody told him any of this."

"Her old boyfriend Alan? Well, you know, people were always coming and going, so by Christmas there might have been a whole new bunch living here. I was out of here by then. Never thought I'd be back, but I heard about this job last year and—" She gave an elaborate shrug. "Hey, it's *temporary.* Just until something happens. You can't give up, you know? You just can't give up and go to friggin' *Fresno,* or Oakville, or wherever the damn place was."

But her words had lost the ring of conviction. She went to find some certainty in the rum bottle, and I let myself out, wondering if my luck would hold and I'd find Crystal up in the Fresno area.

Well, mine did, but I soon found out that Crystal's luck had quickly run out.

I avoided any more nostalgic side trips, found a brand-new Burger King, and used my cell phone to call my assistant, Danny Thu, while I sat in the drive-through and waited for my late lunch. These days I have Danny make computer searches before I undertake any major treks to look for people, especially when the hunt would involve a trip to Fresno in July.

Danny called up an Internet directory that gave two Dalperts in Fresno and one in Oakville, which looked from my three A's map to be a small town about fifteen miles away. None of them had Carl for a first name. After I finished my Whopper, I tried the listing in Oakville first. A man answered and said yes, he was Paul Dalpert.

"I'm looking for *Carl* Dalpert," I said, "and I was wondering if you were related."

There was a moment of heavy silence, then he said, "How did you get this number? Who is this?"

"I found you in the phone directory," I said. "I'm a private investigator and—"

He cut in, demanding, "Is this some kind of sick joke?"

"No, sir," I said. "I would just like to find Carl. Do you know where he is?"

"Yeah, I know," he said harshly. "My son's buried over in St. Michael's Cemetery. Her, too. It's been more than twenty years, lady. I don't appreciate having that mess dug up. So leave us alone, and don't call here again."

Her, too.

I sat for several moments with the disconnect tone humming in my ear, thinking about the last time I'd seen Crystal.

80

It was shortly after graduation, just a brief meeting at the Galleria. She was with a gaggle of friends. I was alone and rushing through some necessary shopping, no mall rat, even then. I'm not sure we said more than hello. But I do remember how she was always in motion, her long blond hair catching the light and the big green eyes alive with excitement.

One of the current favorites in the lexicon of psychobabble is *closure*. I hate the term and think that those who bandy it about so freely understand nothing of the true nature of grief. So I didn't think what I would find up in Oakville would provide any neat ending to Alan Weems' quest. Still, I was getting paid to fill in all the painful blanks, to tidy up all the loose ends. And in this case I had enough personal emotion invested to want to finish the job and do it right.

So even though I could probably have found out by telephone whether Crystal was dead and buried in St. Michael's Cemetery, I left L.A. and drove north through cotton fields, orchards and the simmering heat of the San Joaquin Valley.

There was about an hour of sunlight left when I got to the graveyard just outside Oakville. Even though there was no administration office in the small cemetery, it was easy enough to find Carl. His family had been here long enough to stake out a whole section of plots. But the bright twilight was fading to purple dusk before I found the other marker over in a corner I'd bet was Potter's Field. Just a small rectangular block of concrete set into the earth so a mower could do an unimpeded sweep of the weedy grass. It contained only Crystal's name and nothing else to mark her passing.

With lots of people traveling, I had to settle for an Econo Lodge on Route 99. I was tired, and once in my air-conditioned room, I had no desire to go out in the heat, so I ordered a pizza. While I waited for the delivery, I tried

Mr. Dalpert again. All I got was the answering machine, then and later on my second try. I left polite requests to speak with him about his son and Crystal, not surprised when he didn't call back.

After a restless night listening to the semis highballing it past the motel, I got up early and went to find breakfast and then in search of the details of Crystal's death.

Paul Dalpert was the logical place to start. I located his house about a quarter of a mile up a gravel road just off the highway. It was a square frame, no-nonsense dwelling that must have once been way out in the country and now was right at the city limits. An old Chevy Suburban sat in the driveway. Keeping a wary eye out for dogs, I went to knock on the door. Nobody answered.

Not willing at this point to stake out the place, I wrote a note on one of my cards, telling where I could be reached, stuck it in the screened door and went back into town.

At 9:00 a.m. it was already oppressively hot. The catalpa trees in the small central square were dusty and droopy. Yellowing grass crunched under my feet as I crossed over to city hall, an old two-story stucco building that took up one side of the square.

A clerk told me I'd find death records at the county building over in Fresno. No, sorry, she'd lived in Oakville for only five years, so she knew nothing about anything that had happened before that time.

Well, I knew there was a good-sized newspaper in Fresno where I could also do some research. Before resigning myself to hours of squinting at microfiche, I noted that the local police shared the building, and I thought it couldn't hurt to stop in and ask a few questions.

The police department was housed in an area not much bigger than my two-room office suite back in Santa Ana. A big reception desk took up most of the front room. Behind it, a little tank of a woman was sorting mail. Mid-fifties, I guessed, with short salt-and-pepper hair and rings on almost every finger of her sturdy hands. A plastic sign said she was Delores Krantz.

Two small desks were crammed into the space behind her. One was empty. A young male officer sat at the other, dunking a tea bag in a foam cup and staring glumly at the contents of a thick file folder. Just beyond him a frosted door read Chief of Police.

Ms. Krantz gave me the once-over, and I was sure that regardless of who sat behind that closed door, it was she who really ran the place. I told her what I was looking for, and from the sudden, measuring look in her eyes, I had no doubt she could've told me what I wanted to know.

Instead, she said politely, "I'm sorry, but you'll have to speak to Captain McEndree about that."

But I would not be speaking to him that morning since he was in a meeting with the mayor. There was nothing left but to go on over to Fresno. And for all the information I found there in the official records and old newspaper accounts, I couldn't shake the feeling that only somebody who knew the people involved would be able to tell me what had really happened.

Poor Crystal. She never had a chance to engage in the make-believe violence of films. Instead, she'd found herself involved in the real thing with Carl Dalpert. Their Bonnie-and-Clyde saga had enjoyed front-page coverage in Fresno for only a day, however, before being upstaged by a double homicide involving a city councilman.

From the newspaper accounts and the facts I already knew, I pieced together the story. The trip from L.A. to

Oakville had taken approximately five weeks, a route that began with a jaunt up the coast. There, somewhere around Santa Barbara, Crystal and Carl had added a third person to their party, a young woman named Jolene Walker, and it was Jolene who provided most of the sordid details of what followed.

According to her, she'd been hitching rides, trying to get to San Francisco, when Carl picked her up. Within a day she became a virtual prisoner, fed booze and pills and handcuffed to the bed in various motels and tourist cabins, except when she was taken along on the half dozen armed robberies her captors pulled off as they hopscotched from the coast to the central valley. Lots of lurid sexual innuendo but nothing specific.

For their last hit, Carl targeted a gas station on Highway 41 on the outskirts of Fresno. Big mistake. The owner's son was a California Highway Patrol officer, off duty, helping out his dad.

Again only sketchy details, but a shoot-out took place, during which the patrolman was wounded. Carl and Crystal, dragging Jolene along, ran out and jumped in the car. The officer managed to stagger outside in time to fire at them as they started to speed away, killing Carl. Driverless, the car skidded into a gas pump. Jolene was thrown from the car just before the pump exploded. Somehow the patrolman got Crystal out of the burning vehicle, but she was DOA at the hospital. Jolene suffered a concussion, and it was two days before she regained consciousness.

When she did, the officer corroborated her story of being a victim, remembering the way she had screamed for help as Carl dragged her from the station after the robbery attempt. No charges were filed against her.

The CHP officer's name was Patrick McEndree.

Compared to the picture that had run in that old newspaper account, the sandy hair was a little grayer, and there was a hint of jowls on the handsome face. Still, I thought the years had been kind to Chief of Police Patrick McEndree. He looked like a man who'd made himself a comfortable life and had settled in to enjoy it.

One wall of his office was papered with civic awards, along with several photos of himself as coach of Little League teams, and one of two young look-alikes in uniforms who had to be his sons. There was another picture on his desk, but it was angled so the light reflected off the glass. I got a vague impression of the boys again, this time posed with a woman that I took to be their mother.

"I have to warn you," he said. "My kids and their team are playing Clovis this weekend. I have to get out of here in about fifteen minutes and go practice with them."

He sounded affable enough, but the candid blue eyes were wary and growing a little wintry as I told him of my connection with Crystal and that I was looking for details to fill in what I'd learned.

He said, "If you read the story in the papers, I don't see what else I can tell you."

"Did you try to contact Crystal's family? I know she had an aunt."

"*I* wasn't in charge of the investigation, the county sheriff was. But I'm sure an attempt was made. All we had was her name and that she came from L.A. Maybe you ought to talk to the sheriff."

"I'd like to talk to *you*," I said, "because you were there. Look, the case is closed. It's not like I'm asking for confidential information. I'd just like to understand a little more about what went on during that spree. The whole thing is so out of character for Crystal."

"Yeah, well, Carl's family thought the same thing," he

said dryly. "In their opinion, your friend led their boy astray. But one way or other, Ms. West, you've been in the cop game long enough to know people are totally unpredictable."

He'd checked me out while I was reading old newspaper files. So he was competent if not cooperative.

"Still," I said, "maybe if I could talk to Jolene Walker—do you know what happened to her?"

"Yes, but I'm not going to tell you," he said. "One thing I will say, I know for a fact she can't help you." He put both hands on the desk and pushed himself to his feet.

"You said fifteen minutes."

"I've decided I need to get an early start," he said evenly, coming around the desk and moving over to open the door for me. "Go home, Ms. West. It's an old story, over and done with."

I hated to admit it, but I thought he was right. I stood up, ready to head back to L.A.—and got a good look at the picture on his desk.

"Nice family," I said, trying to cover my hesitation and the sudden leap of knowledge as I stared at the woman in the photo, remembering there had been no pictures of Jolene or Crystal in the old newspaper articles.

Saying, "Thanks for your time," I beat it out of there so I could get to my van before he could leave the station.

Either I did a good job of tailing McEndree or he wasn't as competent as I thought. At any rate, he drove to a house on the edge of town without appearing to make me. Home, I presumed, a nice little ranch house that was old enough so you could tell a room had been added and for some walnut trees to have grown into a shady canopy over the yard. He went inside and reappeared a few minutes later, dressed in jeans and a T-shirt.

Two exuberant young boys bounded out with him. From where I sat in the van half a block away, I could hear their voices, high but still distinctly male, yelling, "Bye, Mom," to the woman who came out to wave them off.

She stood for a few moments, watching them go, long enough for me to get a good look at her face through the zoom lens of my camera. Time might have dimmed the glow, but even without makeup and with the blond hair scraped back in a ponytail, she was still a beautiful woman.

I sighed, put down the camera without taking the picture, and watched her go back in the house. Sat there for a while and weighed my obligation to my client against the bewilderment and pain that my report could bring to those two little boys, a devoted husband and a woman who had made her choices years ago.

Obligations be damned.

I drove away and left Crystal and her family alone.

County records in Fresno confirmed a marriage between Patrick McEndree and Jolene Walker six months after the shoot-out at the gas station. So my hunch was right: McEndree didn't know his wife's real identity. If he had, if he'd been protecting her secret, I'm sure I'd never have gotten a look at that picture on his desk.

Two things seemed obvious to me. One was that it had been Crystal who was victimized by Carl and Jolene on that nightmare trip. The second was that there had been some mix-up about her identity after the aborted robbery when Crystal lay unconscious in the hospital, and that she had gone along with the mistake when she woke up. What I wanted to do was go back, knock on Crystal's door and ask her why. Instead, I headed south to Orange County, trying to decide what to tell Alan.

In the end I endured my twinges of conscience and simply said that Crystal had died in an automobile accident. Alan didn't press for details, saying only that he had to know, and now that he did, he could let her go.

Despite my guilt at lying to a client, I knew I'd done the right thing. Crystal had her own reasons for abandoning her old life. While I'd never know what they were for sure, I could make a few guesses.

Growing up as the prettiest girl in school would have come with the freight of expectations—her own and everybody else's. I'd bet she really believed she was going to take Hollywood by storm. Maybe her rude awakening had also included a flash of the future, a premonition of what her friend Heather had become. Or maybe she just couldn't face admitting failure to her aunt, to Alan, to everybody.

If I gave it some thought, I could come up with some darker scenarios. God knows the Hollywood scene abounded with them.

In any case she'd been desperate enough to go off with Carl Dalpert, a stupid mistake that might have proven fatal. Instead, fate had stepped in to offer her a new life. Well, she'd made her choice just as I'd made mine, and finally I thought I understood why. Because the Crystal Landry whom Alan and I had known really died, along with her Hollywood dreams, not in Fresno but in that old hotel somewhere south of Melrose.

The Sweet Old Lady Who Sits in the Park

Mrs. Hartley settled into a shady corner of the park bench to wait for Mr. Smith. Not his real name, of course. It was a code name she had made up—strictly unnecessary—but besides indulging an old lady's love of intrigue, it served a useful purpose by keeping things at an impersonal level.

The park was a favorite place for the community's older generation to congregate on a sunny afternoon, to play cards and checkers, or simply sit, dozing in the sun. There was plenty of activity to watch if you were interested. The park formed a buffer zone between the northern boundary of the inner city's business district and an old residential neighborhood with a pleasantly homogeneous population.

Mornings, young mothers pushed strollers beneath the elm trees. At lunch time businessmen crossed the park to eat at Fritz's, a restaurant serving both areas of the community. All day long people hurried to appointments and home again.

After four weeks the others had automatically left this particular spot, a bench facing the main walk that bisected the park, except for Mrs. Hartley. She sat and knitted and smiled at everybody who passed. Most of the people smiled back, sometimes adding a cheerful "Hello." A great many of them thought wistfully that all grandmothers ought to be comfortably round with soft white curls, lively eyes, and skin like faded pink silk.

Mrs. Hartley knew the picture she made. To tell the truth she enjoyed it. It was difficult to remind herself that in a few hours her job would be finished and she would never come here again.

I'm getting too old for this, she thought. The argument had been going on for several days inside her head. She had been very careful with her money. After today there would be enough so that she could quit working and find an apartment. Not in this neighborhood, unfortunately, but someplace equally nice. *If inflation doesn't flare up again and eat up my savings,* she amended. *If I don't get sick.*

She hid trembling hands in the blue wool on her lap. No use trying to reason with fear. She had learned when Edward died what it meant to be alone and destitute. It was a lesson she wasn't likely to forget.

"Emma?"

Startled, she looked up to find Jacob Morrison bending over her. "I'm sorry, Jacob. I was far away."

"Not a happy journey, I think." He leaned heavily on his cane as he folded his long body into a sitting position beside her.

For the past week Jacob had stopped to chat briefly before his daily chess game. Today she would have preferred to be alone but she couldn't be unkind to him.

"I was thinking about my husband," she said.

"Ah. You have spoken very little about him. He died of a heart attack, I think you said. It must have been a shock."

"Yes. A great shock."

"What was Mr. Hartley's profession?"

"Edward had his own business. He fixed things." *And so do I. If you knew, Jacob . . .*

"Nice for you. I was never mechanically inclined. My wife, God rest her soul, used to say I was all thumbs. Was he good at his work?"

"Quite good." Dear Edward. There must have been

plenty of money. Not his fault that he was such a poor manager, or that he wanted to give her every luxury.

"I was a musician before my arthritis," Jacob was saying. "Always on the road. At least you had a settled life."

"Not really. Edward's work was specialized and he traveled quite a bit. Since we never had children, I always went along."

"Well, you were lucky to be together."

"Yes, we were."

Especially that last night when Edward had his attack. At the time it had been a shattering experience but later she was thankful that he had died in her arms rather than in a strange room in an indifferent town.

"You'll excuse me, Emma." Jacob pushed himself erect with his cane. "I see my opponent has arrived. Till tomorrow?"

"Till . . ." She stared at him with an overwhelming sense of loss. "Till later."

Now don't you get maudlin, Emma Hartley, she told herself severely as she watched Jacob hobble away.

She pictured cold dark rooms, hunger, the smell of poverty and despair. The vision dispelled any guilt feelings and pulled her up straight on the bench. She had done what she had to do that time eight years ago when Edward died. People were not lining up to offer jobs to fifty-nine-year-old widows with no marketable skills, so she simply took over Edward's business. Thank God he had made notes in his spidery handwriting, enabling her when she finally became desperate to take up where he left off. It still amazed her that she could do the work so efficiently and that it bothered her not at all. After all, men like Mr. Smith . . .

He was coming down the path, briskly as always, looking very *dapper,* to use an old-fashioned and extremely descriptive word. A slim man with ears laid closely against his head, pale blue eyes, and a thin moustache. His charcoal silk suit looked as though it just came out of a cleaner's bag and he always carried, even though it was summer, a pair of thin gray gloves. Another man followed closely behind. Mr. Smith never walked alone. Mrs. Hartley felt a tremor of fear when she saw it was the big man today, the one with enormously muscled shoulders and long, hairy arms. He looked very much like the gorilla in Lincoln Park Zoo, all that brute strength and feral cunning that made you shiver and stand a respectful distance from the cage.

Trying to ignore the quivering in her stomach, Mrs. Hartley stood up and her knitting bag went tumbling, practically beneath the feet of the two men. She herself staggered and would have fallen except that Mr. Smith grabbed her arm to steady her.

"Oh my, how clumsy," Mrs. Hartley cried. "Please excuse me. Sometimes when I stand up suddenly, I get a bit dizzy and . . . Thank you so much," she said as Mr. Smith motioned to the Gorilla Man to pick up her things.

"You all right?" he asked. "Do you need a doctor?"

"Heavens, no. Just a bit wobbly but otherwise I'm perfectly fine." She accepted the tangle of wool offered awkwardly by the Gorilla Man and called, "Goodbye," with a wave as Mr. Smith walked on, a self-satisfied smile hovering on his thin lips.

His good deed for the day, Mrs. Hartley thought dryly, and very few of those to warm his soul. She waited exactly fifteen minutes, packed her knitting bag efficiently, and without the slightest unsteadiness headed toward Fritz's, where Mr. Smith always had his lunch.

The two men were seated at a corner table, a protective wall behind Mr. Smith; the Gorilla Man was positioned so he had a view of the room. He grunted something as Mrs. Hartley swept past the maitre d' straight for their table with excitement coloring her cheeks and shortening her breath.

"I thought you might be here. I'm so glad I caught you." She grabbed the edge of the table for support and put her hand against her throat. "Oh, dear, I—I hurried too fast. Do you suppose I could . . ."

Mr. Smith looked wary and very slightly put upon but he nodded curtly toward a chair and Mrs. Hartley collapsed with a huge sigh. A waiter hurried over. Mr. Smith shook his head but Mrs. Hartley didn't see that. "Some tea would be very nice. You wouldn't mind?" she asked guilelessly.

"No, of course not. Tea," he said sharply to the waiter and fastened his ice-chip eyes on Mrs. Hartley. "Now, was there something you wanted?"

"Of course. You really must think me a silly old woman. First falling all over you and now interrupting your lunch." She opened her handbag. The Gorilla Man stiffened as though ready to lunge across the table, then relaxed when she took out an elegant gray glove. "You dropped this on the sidewalk. Oh, marvelous," she said to the waiter as he put down a steaming pot and cup. He had coffee on the tray and attended to refills.

Mr. Smith pocketed the glove and reached for the sugar bowl. "Thanks for bringing the glove. They're favorites of mine." The graciousness was stilted.

Doesn't have much practice, Mrs. Hartley thought.

She beamed as she poured the tea. "I thought they must be, such lovely leather. I do appreciate beautiful things. Once, well . . ." She didn't notice the look of bored resignation that passed between the two men as she chattered away with the bright intensity of a lonely old lady while she stirred, sipped, wrinkled her nose. "Dear me, I am getting absent-minded. I forgot the sugar."

She put down the cup to reach for the sugar bowl, but failed to put it straight in the saucer. It teetered there and a brush of her sleeve turned it straight toward Mr. Smith's lap. Mrs. Hartley leaped up with a wail, grabbing napkins to mop at the spill but only succeeded in upsetting the Gorilla Man's coffee, too. Both men jumped up to avoid the hot liquid and Mr. Smith swore savagely.

"Get a waiter," he snarled to the Gorilla Man. "Don't stand there like a fool."

Poor Mrs. Hartley had managed some semblance of order by the time the waiter arrived and insisted on helping the man put the table in order. Mr. Smith, disgusted, was ready to leave but by then the food was ready and Mrs. Hartley, flushed with embarrassment and with tears trembling on her lashes, pleaded, "Oh, do sit down and eat. I'd be so upset to know I'd spoilt your lunch. I'm so sorry."

She gathered her things and hurried from the room, pausing only once to make sure he had indeed sat down and, with a final muttered curse, picked up his coffee cup and ordered the waiter to bring the knockwurst.

It was several days before Mrs. Hartley allowed herself to relax. She had gone directly to the airport from the restaurant. A cab was waiting, dispatched according to her earlier instructions, first to the apartment building to pick up her luggage and then to the corner a block from Fritz's. She made the two o'clock flight with minutes to spare. Her only link with Mr. Smith had gone into a trashcan as she walked briskly to her taxi. Mr. Smith had, after all, cooperatively dropped a glove in the park. The pair she bought had not been needed. She doubted that anybody noticed her disposing of them; all their attention had been focused on the sirens screaming through the streets.

And who would attach any importance to the clumsy old woman and the incident preceding Mr. Smith's sudden heart attack? A fast-acting, undetectable drug in his coffee? Nonsense! All that greasy food—cholesterol, the doctors would declare; cholesterol and stress, a deadly combination.

Now, days later and a thousand miles away, Mrs. Hartley sat on a park bench in a shady corner. A palm tree waved overhead and a hummingbird darted in a mass of scarlet hibiscus. She took out her knitting and smiled at everybody who passed. Any minute now she'd have her first glimpse of Mr. Jones. Not his real name, of course, but . . .

It Takes One to Kill One

For most people a daily routine contributes to a happy healthy life. For Emma Hartley such regular patterns of behavior could be fatal.

Perhaps the perfect weather lulled her into complacency. Maybe it was sheer carelessness. In any case, she had fallen into the habit of going for her walk in the beachfront park each morning just after the fog rolled out.

That particular day the Pacific lived up to its name. It lay, flat and peaceful, like an enormous blue-gray lake. Although the air was cool, a warm wash of sunlight filtered through the palm fronds and lacy eucalyptus leaves. She needed only a lightweight pink sweater set over her white knit slacks, and would soon be removing the cardigan.

A popular place, the park's broad asphalt path paralleled the ocean and had a constant flow of joggers, dog walkers, cyclists, and several seniors like herself. Some of them, she noted, trotted along, spry as people half their age.

Observing their exuberance, Mrs. Hartley wistfully considered joining a gym and trimming down. Oh, she could do it if she tried. Even at seventy-two, she was not one to admit to many impossibilities. However, diets and svelte new looks were not really an option for her.

Her ample soft body, her snow-white hair, the sweet, round, dimpled cheeks—in her profession these were valuable assets, so she might as well resign herself to the fact that she would stroll rather than trot.

Distracted by this chain of perfectly normal thoughts and

enjoying the walk and the weather, she certainly wasn't thinking about the dangers of an established routine. So she paid little attention to the man who approached along the path until it was too late.

At the last moment, a little danger flag did go up. Something about the way he moved, or perhaps it was the leather jacket he wore, much too warm for the balmy morning. But to tell the truth she was more concerned with the bicycle coming behind him, pedaled by a young woman going way too fast.

The man was only two steps away from Mrs. Hartley when his lips peeled back in a smirky grin and sunlight glinted on something he took from the inside pocket of the jacket. She recognized the object instantly as a shiny steel ice pick, and she never doubted that it was meant to slide between her ribs and into her heart.

Realizing this, she froze for a fraction of a second. During that instant, that eternity of hyper-sensitivity, she saw the man's rangy strength and dark, stringy hair; smelled his body odor mixed with the aroma of orange peels in a nearby trash can; and heard the cry of seabirds, the clack of bocci balls from the lawn bowling course on the other side of the park, the metallic hiss of the chain on the bicycle rapidly overtaking them both.

Then she moved—surprising both Mr. Ice Pick and herself with her speed. Deliberately, she threw herself out of his path and right in front of the bike. She did this although she was overcome with terror at the thought of splintered hip sockets, of convalescent homes, of long and miserable recoveries.

All things considered, pain and inconvenience was far preferable to death.

Even braced for the impact, the shock of her collision with the bicycle still jarred her spine and sent her flying. She aimed for the grass rather than the asphalt. When she hit the ground, the jolt wasn't nearly as bad as she had anticipated.

All that padding, she observed wryly, had once again served a useful purpose by turning her tumble into a pratfall.

The cyclist went down with her in a tangle of aluminum spokes and tanned young limbs. Somehow Mrs. Hartley managed to avoid the hard protrusions of pedals and handle bars. And the mangled bicycle and its fallen rider provided a blessed barrier between Emma and her would-be assassin.

The man loomed above the women and glared down, a baleful gleam in his eyes. He was clearly not someone who took kindly to being outfoxed. But, for now at least, he had put away the ice pick.

Untangling herself from the bike, the cyclist stared at Mrs. Hartley with alarm. "Oh, my God, are you all right? Are you hurt? Oh, I'm so *sorry*—"

The young woman had two skinned knees herself and a scraped elbow, but she ignored the wounds as she hovered, peering anxiously at Mrs. Hartley.

Emma's main injury was to her dignity, but she moaned loudly and cried, "My back! I hurt my back!"

"Go get help," the cyclist cried to Mr. Ice Pick. "Find a phone. Call nine-one-one. Hurry!"

"My car's right over there," he said. "I could drive her to the hospital a lot faster."

"Are you crazy? We can't move her."

But Mr. Ice Pick ignored the warning. He reached down, seized Mrs. Hartley's wrist, and yanked hard. Emma moaned louder and resisted, turning her extra pounds into dead weight because she was determined not to be taken to this man's car or to wind up any place near the weapon hidden in his jacket.

"Stop it," the young woman warned indignantly. "Let go of her."

Mr. Ice Pick might have ridden roughshod over the woman, jerked Emma up and carried her off. He looked like a man who was used to doing what he pleased no matter what the cost.

But an elderly couple with a small white poodle had stopped, along with a muscular young jogger. Thankfully, they chimed in, agreeing that an injured person shouldn't be moved under any circumstances.

The poodle yapped non-stop, baring his teeth and growling at Mr. Ice Pick. No fooling that intelligent little dog.

Reluctantly, Mr. Ice Pick released Emma's wrist. He did this partly, Emma suspected, because a young patrolman with a hand-held two-way radio was pushing through the gathering crowd.

Another well-modulated moan, and the policeman was on the radio, ordering up the paramedics.

Once at the hospital, Mrs. Hartley's age, her continued complaints of pain, and a very good health plan guaranteed her a night under observation. She didn't see the cyclist in the emergency room, so the young woman's injuries must have been minor.

Emma didn't see Mr. Ice Pick, either.

Maybe I was wrong, she thought as a nice volunteer aide about Emma's own age who said to please call her Donna helped Emma into a wheelchair for the ride upstairs.

The man was probably just some random crazy. Goodness knows, there were plenty of those around. She had jumped to the wrong conclusion, that's all.

She might have convinced herself, except for one thing. Just for an instant before Mr. Ice Pick let her go, he had stared straight into Emma's eyes. Since he was bending down, he was close enough so there was no mistaking the message in that black gaze.

Not madness. No, what she had seen was frustration, pure malevolence, and a savage promise to return and finish what he'd started.

She shivered now, and Donna asked, "Are you all right, love? Are you cold? Should I get you a blanket?"

"Just a goose walking on my grave," Emma said.

Donna gave her a nod and a cheerful smile, never suspecting that the old saying was far from a joke.

Mrs. Hartley and Donna shared the elevator with two men, so young you'd never know they were doctors except for the identification tags pinned to their lab coats.

There was no sign of Mr. Ice Pick in the halls or in any of the waiting areas that they passed. Emma began to breathe a little easier.

It was possible he was leery of coming to the hospital. Certainly he would want to steer clear of the security staff. She might have a short respite, a time to collect her wits and figure out what to do. It might even be wise to talk the doctor into an additional night's stay.

"Well, here we are," Donna announced as she wheeled Emma into her room.

It was spacious enough, as hospital rooms go, with two beds and a window with a view of the parking lot. In the second bed lay a scrawny woman of indeterminate age with a mane of wild mouse-brown hair and pale blue eyes that shone with suspicion and derangement.

"I brought you a roommate, Althea," Donna said. "Isn't that nice?"

"Get out while you can," Althea said darkly. "They do

things to you here. Bad things."

"Oh, my," Donna said. "Somebody didn't take their meds. Don't pay any attention, love," she added to Mrs. Hartley. "She's really a sweet thing."

"I'm sure," Mrs. Hartley murmured.

She had far more to worry about than the poor paranoid woman sharing her room because out in the hall a chillingly familiar figure was strolling past the open door.

Mr. Ice Pick.

He paused for a moment, regarding her with a wolfish grin, then walked on.

The sight of him banished any lingering hope that she had simply crossed paths with a psychopath with a hatred for little old ladies who reminded him of his grandmother.

Somebody had sent him, one of those people who intoned, "An eye for an eye" when they engaged such services. Emma knew from experience how this type of person often used the biblical justification to excuse the exchange of money for a human life.

Donna helped Mrs. Hartley into bed, saying, "Now then, why don't we take a nice little rest?"

A good idea. Emma's knees felt like jelly, and if she had been hooked up to a heart monitor, Donna might have called for a crash cart.

After she was tucked in, Mrs. Hartley lay there, propped up by pillows, taking deep, calming breaths. She was safe enough for the moment with somebody like Althea in the room. Or at least until medication turned the woman into a zombie. And there should be nurses and aides and doctors popping in and out.

But later, in those quiet hours before dawn when it would be very easy for the hit-man to sneak in—well, that would be a different situation.

"I'm telling you," Althea warned in ominous tones, "we'll never get out of this place alive."

"You may be right, my dear," Emma said. "You may be right."

Blood pressure checks, more prodding and poking, little white paper cups with pills. Althea's medicine turned her dreamy and docile just as Emma feared. Emma was given a muscle relaxant, which she spit out as soon as the nurse turned away.

Relaxing was a luxury she could not afford, not even for a second.

Even though she appreciated the security aspect of all the activity, it would have been nice to have some uninterrupted time to consider her options. Clear thinking was a necessity now; her life depended on it.

An ordinary person would just call the police. For Emma Hartley this was out of the question, and of course Mr. Ice Pick knew it.

The safest and most logical thing to do was to try and slip out of the hospital without him seeing her. Assuming this was possible—an optimistic assumption—she could simply make her escape, leave town, and disappear. With luck Mr. Ice Pick or somebody like him would never find her.

But did she really want to live that way, constantly looking over her shoulder? She thought not.

To tell the truth she was tired of a nomadic life. She had enjoyed the traveling during her marriage. She and Edward were constantly on the road while he attended to the jobs he referred to as trouble-shooting. He had never wanted to talk about his work, and she never pressed. If she had her suspicions, she ignored them. Then, some fourteen years ago, Edward suffered a sudden heart attack and died.

Suddenly she was faced with several grim realities: There was barely enough money to bury her husband and pay the hotel bills; he had left her with no savings and very little life insurance; and his line of work would not generate social security payments. His only legacy had been a journal detailing every aspect of his profession.

Fortunately, she found she had a talent for the business and a pragmatic outlook. Emma Hartley also prided herself on accepting only assignments that would rid society of individuals who were the equivalent of cockroaches and accomplishing these jobs with a certain dispassionate finesse.

With plenty of vermin in the world, over the years she had accumulated a nice little nest egg. Her savings allowed her to come to this California seaside town and buy some property for a permanent base, maybe even to consider retiring. Not one to rush into things, she'd rented a house first, month-to-month, while she looked for just the right place.

Now those plans were, as they say on TV, in the dumper. She would have to take care of Mr. Ice Pick first and then find some other place to settle down, this time with the proper precaution.

After her nap, the dinner trays arrived. "Direct from Spago's," the young aide said, removing the plastic cover with a flourish to reveal plain meatloaf and mashed potatoes.

Well, the meal wasn't gourmet, but it was tasty enough, and Emma needed to keep up her strength so she ate every bite.

Afterward, with the staff busy picking up trays and Althea studying her hands with dreamy concentration, Emma called and arranged for a taxi. She had never learned to drive, and, although Californians seemed to view cabs as undependable exotica, she found them just as convenient here as any place.

Then she rested and waited for the taking of temperatures

and the dispensing of medications and for the eleven o'clock shift change.

By midnight Althea had drifted off into a drugged sleep. Mrs. Hartley was so tired herself that it was a terrible temptation to close her eyes, just for a few minutes. But the prospect of awakening to Mr. Ice Pick's face leering down gave her plenty of impetus to get moving.

Better tired than dead, she told herself sternly.

Dressing was harder than she expected. Her muscles were sore, and her joints had stiffened up from the fall. She placed pillows under the thin blanket to approximate her plump shape. An old trick, but one that might buy her a minute or two.

Then she slipped out into the hall and went down the corridor, on the alert for the enemy. He was nowhere to be seen. This didn't surprise Emma. Mr. Ice Pick was not the type who could lurk around unnoticed. He'd have to find a hiding place or else leave the hospital with a plan to gain entrance later on.

She decided to spend a few minutes scouting and found a fire door wedged open. A roof access, she supposed. Perhaps he was out there, waiting. She certainly wasn't about to confirm her suspicions.

The taxi sat at the designated spot, driven by a nice man who indulged her vague directions, which sent him doubling back and forth—until she was certain that nobody was following.

If anybody asked, the driver might remember her, but she doubted there'd be all that much fuss about an old lady who wandered away from the hospital, one who had no relatives or friends to press for a search.

She had the driver drop her off a block from her rental house and approached it cautiously just in case Mr. Ice Pick had anticipated her plans. He looked the Neanderthal type, more brawn than brain, but it never paid to underestimate.

The short block seemed a mile long and full of threatening shadows. Well, at least she was wide awake from all the adrenaline by the time she let herself into the house.

Inside, she hustled around as fast as her tender muscles permitted. Very soon now Mr. Ice Pick would be sneaking into her room at the hospital. Time was slipping away.

After changing into a warm velour sweat suit, she collected a blanket, her hair dryer, a hammer, some wire, and a few other things. These she took along with a big, bright flashlight and went out by the pool.

After going over the plan once again in her mind, she lit only one of the tiki torches, selecting it carefully, then set everything else up accordingly.

With all that accomplished, she positioned a lawn chair on the far side of the pool and settled down to wait with the blanket over her knees. By then the fog had moved in, blotting out the stars.

Once in a while she caught a glimpse of the moon, a dim, watery disk quickly lost in drifting gray clouds. The air was growing chill, but she was quite comfortable, although she found herself longing for a peppermint schnapps.

Near the pool a lime tree bloomed, exuding a sweet, heavy perfume. A nightbird peeped in the bushes, and traffic droned in the distance.

She had positioned her lawn chair, lit by the single tiki torch, to direct attention to herself while the rest of the yard stayed in dense shadow. The remainder of the outdoor furniture was only a group of vague shapes.

With its retractable cover closed, the small pool was an indistinct oval and blended in with the concrete apron of the patio, at least in the darkness. The cover was meant to keep out leaves and conserve the warmth. The rental agent had also assured Emma it was strong enough for safety's sake to walk on.

Looking around, Emma felt a pang of regret. Really a lovely backyard, very private. A hill rose behind the house, putting enough distance between it and the homes above so that one barely knew they were there. As for the houses on either side, one was occupied by a young man who worked nights, the other by a middle-aged couple who traveled extensively. They had just left for Hong Kong.

During the past few weeks, Emma had grown to like the place and had even thought of buying it, an impossibility now, thanks to Mr. Ice Pick.

She had no doubt he would come. If he'd found her in the park, he must know where she lived. And, when he discovered her hospital bed empty, this was the next logical place to check.

A few more minutes and she saw a firefly flicker of light in the house. She sat straighter, heart drumming, her mouth dry, and picked up the flashlight. The sliding patio door gave a metallic squeal, and then she saw his bulky shape slip outside.

She had a terrible moment when she was sure she'd miscalculated, that he had a gun and would simply blast her and run for it. But old habits die hard, she'd counted on that, that and his fear of the noise. He didn't know about the neighborhood, after all. And when she hit him with the powerful flashlight beam, she saw with relief that he carried only the ice pick.

He put his hand up against the glare, blinking, muttering, "What the *hell*—"

She shut off the light now that it had done its part by temporarily blinding him.

Keep walking, she thought while he hesitated.

"I knew you'd come," she said, making her voice shaky, hopeless, and resigned.

"Smart for an old broad," he said and took a step or two toward her.

"I was going to run, but I'm too old and tired." she said. "I knew you'd only catch me."

"Yeah? You got that right." A few more wary steps.

"Just one question—please," she said. "Who sent you? Can you tell me that much?"

"Sure. Said to tell you the Blackbird. Said he wanted you to know."

How long for his eyes to adjust? He began to skirt left around the pool, maybe sensing it was there even if he didn't see it. She gave a little moan and got up, backing away as though fear had gotten the better of her after all.

He cursed and changed his angle to come toward her, now coming at a fast lope. This course put him on the pool cover, which she had left open about two feet at the deep end. She switched on the flashlight, giving him another blast of light in case his eyes were adjusting.

He was near enough so she could see the realization on his face that something was wrong here, very wrong, but it was too late.

His foot hit the trip wire, which she had strung across the pool. He fell with a splash into the open space. In the beam of the flashlight, she saw him recover quickly. He coughed, roared more curses, and grabbed for the edge of the cover. But she was already reaching for the extension cord, a nice, sturdy outlet strip with a rocker switch.

Earlier she had plugged her hair dryer into the outlet strip, then dropped the dryer into the pool. Now, in the water, the dryer made a sound something like a king-size bug zapper.

She turned off the flashlight, not really wanting to see his body twitching with the electric shock. She certainly didn't want to touch him to see if he was dead. When he grew still, she simply turned off the rocker switch, removed the dryer, and closed the stout pool cover.

By then she really did need her peppermint schnapps, so she blew out the tiki torch and went inside for a double shot before she called a cab.

On a redeye flight leaving Los Angeles, Mrs. Hartley promised herself to be more cautious from now on. This time she'd been very lucky that things had worked so well.

She'd had a few misgivings about the amount of water in the pool versus the current generated by the small hair dryer even though Edward had written in his journal about once using such a tactic, citing the conductivity of natural minerals in the water and the fact that pool plumbing provided a ground. She was only glad she hadn't been forced to use the hammer she'd hidden in the bushes.

In fifteen days when her lease expired, she doubted the police would connect the old lady who rented the house with the old lady who wandered off from the hospital. If they did, Mrs. Hartley felt sure they'd expect her to be another victim, not the one responsible for the bloated horror they would find in the pool.

As for Mr. Ice Pick—good riddance. Even though she and this thug were, theoretically, in the same business, the difference was she did not relish taking a life. Her would-be assassin had no such moral compunction; remembering his grin on the path in the park, she knew he actually enjoyed his work.

She tucked in the airline blanket, positioned the little pillow for lumbar support, and settled back. The lights were off in the cabin, and it was quiet except for the throbbing roar of the jet engines. A perfect place for thinking, and what she thought about was Mr. Ice Pick's boss.

Somehow he must have discovered Emma's part in eliminating his head enforcer in the loan-sharking division two years ago. Mr. Blackbird was careful as well as dangerous. Too bad he was so old-fashioned, sending his nickname so she would know who was responsible for her death.

She knew who he was, of course. She had made it her business to find out all about him before accepting the assignment. Now she recalled all those details and made a few plans.

Then she pulled the airline blanket around her and closed her eyes. It had been an exhausting day. She really needed a nap.

Before she fell asleep, she thought again about Florida. Sarasota, perhaps, or Fort Meyers, both would be nice places to settle down.

Yes, Florida would be her final destination. But that would come later, after this trip to Cleveland where she intended to pay Mr. Blackbird a call.

Sorry, Frank

Mrs. Scoville? This is Memorial Hospital. Your husband was in an accident and I'm afraid he's in critical condition. Could you come down right away? I think you'd better hurry . . .

"Ethel!"

The coffeepot slipped out of her hands, splashing water and carefully measured coffee into the sink and staining her yellow robe.

"I can't find the mouthwash. Where is it? Did you forget to buy it again?"

She closed her eyes and gripped the counter to keep her voice quite detached. "I'm sorry, Frank. I'll get some today."

He stomped into the kitchen wiping the perspiration already filming his beefy face. "Sorry, Frank," he mimicked. "Always excuses. You never remember a thing. Where's my coffee? Didn't you even start it yet?"

Her numb fingers reassembled the coffeepot and plugged it in. She watched nervously as it gurgled, and tried to remember how much coffee she had put in.

"Ethel!"

"Right away, Frank." She hurriedly put his eggs and toast on a plate, wincing at the sight of the egg yolk broken in her haste. He shot her a murderous look but began eating without comment. She went to get his coffee as Janey walked in, smiling a sleepy hello. Ethel opened her mouth in warning, but it was too late.

"Ethel! Look at this kid. Are you letting her go to school looking like that?"

110

Janey appealed mutely to her mother. "Frank," Ethel began timorously, "all the girls wear short skirts—"

"I don't care what other girls wear. My daughter's not going around looking like that. Why, she might as well go out in her underwear and be done with it. Ethel!"

"Go change your clothes," Ethel said.

"But, Mother—" Tears edged Janey's plea.

"You heard your father," Ethel said harshly, her stomach twisting into knots. "Now go on, do as I say."

"Ethel! For heaven's sake! Where's my coffee?"

She poured it quickly, sloshing some of the hot liquid on her hand and biting her lip to keep from crying out.

He gulped it down, making a face, his complaints cut short by a horn sounding out front. Thrusting the cup at her, he rushed out yelling over his shoulder, "Don't forget to iron some shirts today."

She sank down at the table with tension vibrating her heart like a drum.

Mrs. Scoville? This is Henry Miller down at the plant. I'm awful sorry to be the one to tell you—it's Frank, Mrs. Scoville. He's had a heart attack. They're taking him to the hospital, and, well, it's pretty bad. I think you'd better get over there right away . . .

"Mother," Janey said, "is this okay?"

Ethel nodded vaguely. The red skirt had been exchanged for a blue one just as short as the original. A sly flicker of triumph shone briefly on Janey's face.

Maybe I was wrong, Ethel thought dully as Janey gulped her breakfast and hurried off to school. *All these years I stayed with Frank, for Janey's sake. She needs a father; but lately . . .*

She poured herself a cup of the muddy coffee. Fourteen years ago Frank Scoville burst like an energetic whirlwind into her quiet life, sweeping her into marriage. He radiated

111

self-confidence, and his aggressiveness—well, he needed that to get ahead in the brilliant future she could see as clearly as a road map.

The vision of success faded slowly over the years, the opportunities slipping away from his frustrated grasp. Of course there was always somebody to blame: the boss's brother nosing him out of the promotion, the office manager jealous of Frank's brilliance, and always holding him back was Ethel—a handy scapegoat for all the things that happened with nobody handy to blame. His constant belittlement changed her gentle humor into mute silence and her slight forgetfulness into complete disorganization.

Mrs. Scoville? This is the Los Angeles Police Department. Sorry to have to tell you this, ma'am. A holdup was in progress at the bank this morning when your husband walked in. There was some shooting. He's still alive but I think you'd better get to the hospital right away . . .

The telephone rang, jolting her out of the daydream. Her eyes focused guiltily on the clock. "Eleven!" She hurried to pick up the phone.

"Ethel! Where were you? You go back to bed?"

The kitchen littered with dirty dishes, the beds unmade, his shirts left to iron, the shopping to do—all of it began closing in on her. "What is it, Frank?"

"I want you to take the car by the garage and have them check out the brakes. You understand?"

"Today? But, Frank, I'm supposed to go to school. The PTA Board—"

"Look, hang the PTA. Damn waste of time anyway. I have to use the car tomorrow to call on some customers up in Hollywood and the brakes feel funny. I don't want to drive up and down all those hills without having them checked. Ethel!"

"Yes, Frank," she said tiredly, hanging up the phone.

Another missed meeting, she thought. It had taken all her courage to say yes when asked to serve on the Board, knowing full well they must have been scraping the bottom of the barrel when they called her. She had begun to enjoy it, but now it was just like the Reading Club and the Brownies when Janey was small. Always there was something to keep her away; something for Frank more important than her own pitiful attempts for an outside interest.

"Eleven-thirty!" She started cleaning feverishly. If she hurried—the meeting was at two; maybe, just maybe . . .

The meeting ended late and the drumbeat of tension knotted Ethel's stomach around the half of a sandwich and the coffee she'd gulped before she came. It was difficult to concentrate on Gladys Webb's remarks about plans for the Sock Hop with the list of things left to do dancing around in her head. Frank's shirts, the car, and—oh, no, she had forgotten his mouthwash. She fought the late afternoon traffic back to the discount supermarket and stood in line for an interminable time.

It was after four as she headed for home, her head aching fiercely and exhaustion making every turn of the wheel an effort. As she sailed past the service station, she remembered Frank's call and hesitated. "No," she thought, "there's not time, and anyway he'll never know the difference." She switched on the radio defiantly and drove home.

A late bulletin. In Los Angeles today a sniper began firing at random into the street, killing four persons and wounding three others. Among the dead are Mr. Frank Scoville of . . .

A blare of rock music roused her in time to turn into her driveway where the car swayed to a stop just short of the garage door. Trembling, she pushed the guilty panic aside and hurried into the kitchen to put the roast in the oven.

For once it was rare the way Frank liked it; but tough, as he proved by elaborate sawing motions with his knife. She had forgotten all about dessert, and with a martyred air he ate the ice cream she served.

There was a bad moment when he asked about the car, but he accepted her vague answer without question and went to sit in front of the television set. Finally the day dragged to an end.

Fatigue clouded Ethel's mind, but once in bed she tossed fitfully, deep sleep seeming to come only minutes before the alarm rang. She dragged herself into the kitchen and began to fumble with the coffeepot.

"Ethel!" His scandalized voice bellowed. "You forgot to iron my shirts!"

"Yes, Frank, I'll do it right away."

She got a shirt done somehow, took it to him and came back to the kitchen to realize she had forgotten to plug in the coffeepot.

"Ethel! Where's my coffee? Is it too much to ask—hey, look at that kid's hair. I want it cut today, do you hear? Looks like a stringy mop. And I need some foot powder—you'll have to take the bus."

At last he was gone and Janey's wails quieted and Ethel was left to face the dirty kitchen and the weak coffee. She sat down unfeeling, her thoughts drifting, jumbled—*Mrs. Scoville, your husband . . . accident . . . riot . . . heart attack . . . dead . . . dead . . .*

The phone shrilled several times before it penetrated the protective fog. The voice sounded familiar somehow. "Mrs. Scoville, this is Dr. Kline at Memorial Hospital. I'm sorry to have to tell you, but your husband was in an automobile accident, and he's here now in critical condition. A police car is coming to pick you up and bring you here. Mrs. Scoville? Mrs. Scoville?"

She hung up the phone.

Minutes later a pounding on the front door snapped her to her feet. "Eleven o'clock . . ." She stumbled to the sink and began frantically to clean the kitchen. So many things to do . . . the floor . . . how long since she washed it? And Janey's hair . . . maybe if she trimmed it just a little . . .

An Insignificant Crime

When the shop bell rang, I looked up from the account books and groaned. I had enough trouble managing the old man lately without that woman coming around to ruin things completely.

He watched her grimly, his mouth thinned to a tight, self-righteous line—judge, jury, and executioner. I closed the books and hurried to the end of the counter.

"Father, please," I said.

"Please nothing. I meant what I said. If that woman steals something today, I'll turn her over to the authorities."

I kept my voice low, but his was rising in agitation. "Let's go back into the office and talk," I urged quietly. A glassed-in area lay directly behind the counter where it was possible to work and watch the aisles at the same time. He hung back stubbornly, but I coaxed him in and closed the door.

"There's no reason to discuss it," he said.

"There's every reason. Her father has a lot of influence in this town. If you think you can humiliate him without reprisal, you're dangerously mistaken. If she takes something, why can't you simply charge it to his account as you've done in the past?"

"Because it's wrong, that's why. I've compromised my principles long enough."

I began to sweat. The room was oppressively hot but that was only partly the reason. I was shaking with inner rage. The old fool couldn't see beyond the end of his thin quivering nose. He would sacrifice the business and our future, his daughter's and mine, and feel smugly sanctimonious. And for what? An insignificant little crime that would hurt nobody.

"You mustn't judge the poor woman," I said, trying to think of a way to avoid the clash that was sure to come. "Her father says it's a sickness."

"Rubbish. She's a thief, and worse, she makes no attempt to hide it." His jaw set obstinately. There was not a drop of perspiration on that cold forehead. "I tell you I have my principles, though your generation wouldn't understand that. All you value is the dollar."

You should talk, I thought grimly. I've worked for him long enough to know how he cheats his customers. Nothing big or obvious—just a niggling penny here and there or merchandise a bit substandard. My one comfort was that he could not live forever. My wife was his only child, born late. If I hung on, the store would eventually be mine—a starting point for the ideas and plans that churned impatiently inside my head. I couldn't allow him to throw everything away because of his single-minded morality.

He kept watch like a hangman waiting on the scaffold, but I began to feel a little hope. She walked up and down the aisles fingering things and dropping them back in the bins. Perhaps the whole thing would blow over. She didn't *always* steal. It's the weather, I told myself. For weeks the heat had clamped down like the lid on a boiling pot, shredding nerves and stoking tempers. Go away, I pleaded silently; make your purchase and get out of here.

It was too late for prayers. Her plump fingers had chosen their prize for the day, bold as brass. The old man sucked in his breath sharply and prepared to charge out of the office, but I grabbed him.

"I won't let you do this," I said.

"You can't stop me." He tried to shake me off but I hung

on tenaciously. "This is my store. I know you're waiting anxiously for me to die so you can get your hands on it, but at present I am very much alive and I'll do as I please."

"Go ahead then," I said recklessly, "but listen carefully. If you do this, I'm leaving. You spend a lot of time belittling me, but you're not a stupid man. You're crafty enough to recognize the amount of work I put into this store. The truth is, you can no longer handle the business alone."

"Don't be ridiculous," he snapped, but he hesitated.

"I have another opportunity." It was a blatant lie, but I was desperate. "I'll take it tomorrow. You'll lose not only my help but your daughter and grandson as well."

He licked his lips, but I could read nothing in those hooded, fish-gray eyes. It took every ounce of my willpower to fold my arms and lean casually against a desk, to pretend I could breathe the hot soggy air.

"Well," I said. "Exactly how much are your principles worth to you?"

He didn't answer, just turned his back on me and went out to the counter where the woman waited with a few pennies' worth of nails to legitimatize her visit. I thought his walk seemed slower than usual and his shoulders drooped, but I couldn't be certain. I followed him with my heart thudding painfully against my ribs, convinced that I had made a ghastly mistake and ruined my future.

He accepted payment without a word or a look at her large shopping basket where the hatchet handle was plainly visible. He even managed a stiff nod and a "Good afternoon, Miss Lizzie," while I breathed a shaky, victorious sigh and made a note to charge the stolen ax to Mr. Borden's account.

Exit

As Diane swung down the on ramp, she saw the digital dash-
board clock flick from 12:38 to 12:39. Her stomach lurched,
a hollow dropping away like standing on a high building and
looking down. She knew she'd left the theater at 12:10.
Twenty-nine minutes—and only three blocks to the freeway.

Another chunk of her life missing. And unless she could
fill in those lost minutes, they'd be gone for good.

She maneuvered into the traffic. Past midnight but still so
many cars, their headlights lasering off the side mirror into
her eyes. It had been 12:10 when she finished closing and left.
She remembered looking at the clock over the concession
stand. So—five minutes to leave the deserted mall and cross
the enormous parking lot, she certainly remembered that, the
asphalt bathed in yellow light, the edgy crawl of fear from
being out there alone. Damn Mario and Frank had parked on
the other side and hadn't volunteered to walk her to her car.
Just once, *once,* why couldn't Joel offer to come drive her
home? She'd gladly take a bus up or bum a ride, but it never
occurred to him. He had his nine-to-five job and he needed
his rest.

And he could snore through anything: David Letterman,
her insomniac prowlings around the tiny condo, while she
awoke instantly when he got out of bed in the mornings and
never could go back to sleep.

No wonder fatigue clouded her mind so she remembered
only bits and pieces of those twenty-nine minutes: finding
herself on the mall's peripheral road that dead-ended so she

had to backtrack, traffic lights all red and sitting stupidly waiting even though she could legally turn right, the left arrow at the freeway entrance taking forever, then finally going down the ramp and the kid standing there with his thumb out . . . oh yes, she remembered that because he'd been there before, all three nights this week, a skinny, long-legged boy wearing jeans and a black leather jacket.

Dumb kid, probably hitching home from a night job like hers, only who in their right mind would pick him up? And why hadn't the CHP noticed him there, chased him away?

"Looks like we'll make it tonight," the kid said.

She swerved, felt the bump of the lane divider buttons under her wheels and heard a braying horn, swerved back. Her heart thundered, beating so hard she could feel the pounding in the back of her throat and up in her ears. The hitchhiker sat beside her, not so young, she could see that now in the blue glow of the dash lights. A cynical weathered face beneath the lank blond hair, old eyes.

"Don't you think so?" he asked.

"What?" she said faintly.

"That we'll get through before they close the freeway."

I-5 was shut down every night now for the construction that would double its width. She never remembered the closure either and several times got stuck in a jam of cars snaking along a circuitous detour in Irvine.

"I don't know." She must have braked, pulled onto the shoulder, waited for him to run up to the car and climb in, but the memory was gone, gone—"Where did you say you were going?"

A quick gleam of teeth as he smiled. "You'll know when we get there."

A bulldozed shopping plaza, a ditch along one of the remaining strawberry fields. Cars all around but her Camry might as well have been a space capsule hurtling through the stars.

Ahead the freeway curved right around a concrete barricade. Bridge pilings bared jagged rebar teeth. An alien landscape of rubble and gouged earth, mounds of gravel—*God in heaven, where am I?*

Going home, of course, dead tired, with Mr. Stranger Danger in her car. She'd get off at El Toro Road, drive into the first service station, or Don Jose's, or anything that was open. Scream her head off. Run to a phone and call Joel. *Goddamn you, Joel, sound asleep.* He wouldn't even pick up the receiver. He'd let the machine answer.

"There's no need to be nervous," her passenger said.

"I can't help it," she said. "It's not like me, picking up a stranger."

Stopping for him couldn't have been a rational choice. Even if she couldn't remember it, the action had to have been an impulse. But then nothing in her life was rational any more. Events swept her along, the crest of a flood riding above murky, secretive waters.

Exhaustion was a big part of it. Worse, though, every time she walked into the theater, she felt the steel jaws of a trap snapping shut. Besides the hours there was all the political infighting, so intense you'd think the place was a high stakes corporate jungle instead of a shitty little six-plex with crummy wages. She'd tried to find another job. She'd tried to go back to school, quickly finding it impossible to juggle classes around her changing schedule. Joel got good steady raises, but he'd wanted the vacation in Cancun last winter, a BMW—low-end model but essential for his image. Now he said they had to buy a house, get into the real estate market even if it was a stretch, so she couldn't even think of quitting. God knows she couldn't think of having a baby. What she did think of—what she thought of a lot—was just leaving some night, of going—somewhere.

Brakelights flared. Traffic slowed, crawling around another barricade. Up ahead she could see the monolithic rise of bridge supports and the truncated sweep of a new exit ramp encased in wood bracing.

From the passenger seat, the man watched her. How could she have thought he was a kid? His face was carved bone and ancient shadows.

"I'm sorry, I've made a mistake." She was stopped in the lane along the right shoulder. "Please—I'd like you to get out here."

"I don't think so." There was an odd gentleness in his voice. "Don't be afraid, Diane. It's really the best thing."

Diane. When had she told him her name? When she picked him up—no, now she remembered, and she hadn't picked him up. He'd been there in the parking lot and they had talked . . . She felt suddenly calm, calmer than she had in a long time. As some invisible blockage cleared and the traffic speeded off, she accelerated smoothly, a tiny bud of anticipation opening up.

Just ahead the dark exit ramp winged up toward the inky sky. Her passenger didn't have to say a thing because she was already veering right, and for an instant she saw the ramp finished, a solid arc, sodium vapor lamps washing the new white concrete with pale sulphur, going—nowhere . . . which seemed to Diane the logical place to go.

Wolf Winter

Montana Territory, 1885

Allie Reems awoke to a soft chuff of snow sliding from the
eaves and the great white eye of the moon shining in through
a crack in the shutters. She had no idea how long she'd slept.
Across the room the fire had died to ashy embers, and she
could feel the cold air sharp in her lungs.

And then she heard the sound again.

Snow moving. A creak of roof timbers.

During the past three days the wind had howled relent-
lessly down from Canada, changing the face of the wintry
landscape like a deranged sculptor. Drifts built along the
northern side of the cabin, and the wolf had used that great
white dune as a walkway.

He was up above Allie now, prowling the slope of the roof.
Lying in the darkness, she plotted his course. Her heart thundered, and her breath hung in ghostly plumes. He must easily
weigh a hundred and fifty pounds. Was the roof sturdy
enough to hold him?

There was no cushion of attic and rafters, just the cross
members and the peeled saplings that supported rough,
tarred shingles. Still, although Cyrus had never troubled himself about the appearance of things, he had built for perma-
nence, and he, himself, had climbed around up there last fall,
routing a raccoon who tried to make a den beneath the
chimney flashing.

So the wolf would not come crashing through. And the

only other way into the room was through the narrow chimney, which was too narrow for the broad shoulders and deep chest. Just to be sure, she must get up and start the fire. Not only to frighten the wolf. She was warm now beneath a mound of quilts, but soon the covers would be inadequate for the plummeting temperature.

She got up, wrapping a quilt around her shoulders, shivering. As she moved toward the fireplace, the wolf tracked her, matching her steps, his footfalls muffled by the snow on the roof. Her nape hair bristled and her hands shook as she added kindling and coaxed the coals to flame.

She heard his startled scramble when smoke lofted up the chimney, knew he was gone because she felt a release of pressure as though she had been carrying the weight of the animal on her chest.

The door was barred. So were the windows. She picked up Cyrus's Winchester anyway and took it with her as she went to crack a shutter and stare out at the moonlit, crystalline night.

The wolf stood a hundred feet away in the clearing between the old sod shanty and the woods. White on white with just a tracery of gray to delineate the big powerful body. So bright out she could see his snout parted in a wolf grin, the gleaming teeth.

She was a good shot. If she moved quickly, threw open the window . . . She gripped the rifle stock, anticipating the recoil against her shoulder, the sight of the wolf twisting from the impact of the bullet. The moon-black stain on the snow spreading beneath his body.

She reached out and pushed the shutter, her fingers brushing the latch, the metal so cold it was like touching flame. She jerked away. The wolf watched from the clearing, unmoving. Behind her the fire leaped and crackled.

Run, she called silently and after a moment he obeyed, moving effortlessly away into the trees.

The wolf pack had come two years before at the time Cyrus finished the cabin and they moved out of the sod house. Up here, on the edge of the great prairie, the grass didn't produce the thick mass of roots that bound the soil into a fibrous block, so the soddy provided crude shelter at best. She had been so happy walking around the one enormous room of the cabin with the stone fireplace and two shuttered windows that could be thrown open to let in the air and light. She was sure the headaches would go away now, that the sieges had been brought on by the cramped, dark, cave-like house, which was always damp and smelled of the grave.

Ruthie and Joel had scampered around, forever underfoot, while she helped Cyrus move the few pieces of furniture in. They had left St. Joseph with a full wagon of belongings, but most of the items had been bartered away for flour and beans and coffee, the dining room table and chairs simply left beside the road to lighten the load when one of the mules died.

Through everything she'd hung on to the walnut chest of drawers that had belonged to her mother and her grandmother before that. The feel of the satiny wood as she polished it with beeswax reminded Allie of the pleasant life she'd once had and might, someday, make for her children. The dream didn't seem impossible that day as they positioned the chest in the place of honor. They had twenty head of cattle, ten of the cows ready to calve, and a good crop of corn that had survived the depredations of deer and rabbit.

Then, that first night in the new house, the wolves began to howl, their eerie cries bringing her bolt upright, her heart pounding, while Cyrus rolled out of bed, swearing, reaching for his rifle.

A blast of gunfire drove them away, but they always came back. Just their luck, Cyrus said bitterly. Most of the packs had been harvested by trappers or else driven up into Canada.

She never saw the wolves, none of them did, except one night, when her head hurt too badly for sleep, she thought she saw a dark shadow move along the edge of the moonlit woods.

Mostly Joel was out of the house all day. He was eight, old enough to help his father with the cattle and the corn. Four-year-old Ruth stayed close to Allie. She was already a willing little worker, assisting with the endless chores, but her constant childish prattle sometimes drummed Allie's headaches to life. Once started, the long summer twilights, all that endless light, honed the pain to a razored intensity. At such times, when they gathered for meals and their voices assaulted her like hammers, Allie clenched her fists so hard to keep from screaming that her nails left small, bloody crescents in her callused palms.

Late that summer the wolves killed a calf, a stunted runt of an animal. Allie was sure the little heifer would've died anyway, but Cyrus roared with fury. The next time he went to town, he bought two shiny steel traps. Three days later he caught a young bitch, skinned the animal in the woods and brought home the gory pelt.

Allie and the children were down at the creek fetching water for the garden when Cyrus arrived with his trophy. He tossed the skin on the floor beside the front door before he came to get them, his face flushed with triumph as he recounted the kill.

She never forgot the wild blood stench or the hive of flies working on the shreds of wolf flesh. Although she scrubbed the boards until her hands were raw, the odor lingered for days, setting off a headache that blinded her with agony.

Allie worried about the children blundering into the traps, but Cyrus brushed off her concern. He pointed out that Ruthie always stuck to her mother like a cocklebur. And Joel knew where the traps were laid since he helped his father set them, his excitement bright as fever over the kills.

Cyrus built a lean-to next to the sod house to serve as a barn and a split rail fence to keep the young animals safe, and often he would sleep beside the pen with his gun. For several weeks the wolves vanished. Cyrus felt secure enough so that they all rode into town.

Usually, Allie loved the infrequent visits. She had been an outgoing child raised in a sociable family. Enduring the isolation of frontier living, she ached for laughter, fiddle music, the chatter of women. But the light that day seemed abnormally bright, reflecting off all the windows and the shiny tin washtubs that hung outside the general store, and her head rang with the clatter of wagon wheels, the cries of children and the terrible, crashing gong of the blacksmith's mallet striking iron.

She needed no urging from Cyrus to visit the doctor. There, the closed warmth of the tiny office and the smell of iodine and camphor intensified the pain so that by the time she had to suffer his questions and his touch, his face swam in spangled light and her head pulsed with agony.

"I'm afraid I have no cure for you, Mrs. Reems," the doctor said. "I suggest regular meals and regular elimination. And prayer, of course."

"I thought, perhaps, laudanum," she said timidly.

"Never," he declared. "The stuff is habit-forming and I will not prescribe it. Think of the pain as the cleansing hand of God, Mrs. Reems, and I guarantee it will be easier to endure."

Blessedly, she fainted in the wagon on the way home.

Snow magnified the sunshine to white-hot brilliance. Shafts of light blazed in through the joints of the shutters. Allie stuffed clothing around the openings—her own skirts, not Joel's shirts or Ruthie's dresses—but the walls themselves seemed to glow, and she finally crouched in the darkest corner beneath a quilt while the pain raged.

Night brought little relief. Only the icy chill in the cabin drove her up to fumble with kindling and the last of the firewood she'd brought inside before the storm. The room stank of the chamber pot, but she dared not risk a trip outside.

Half a haunch of venison remained in the larder along with a small store of potatoes and turnips. She knew she should eat, but her stomach turned at the thought of food. She huddled before the hearth, listening for heavy footfalls overhead. There was only the quiet shifting of snow in the windless night and the throbbing of her own heart.

That fall the wolves killed two sickly calves and an old cow; Cyrus took three more skins. Tit for tat, he said. These were young animals. The older ones had learned caution and avoided the traps. He added the pelts to two others he had stored out in the sod house until he could take them to town, but she still smelled the dark rancid stink.

Allie broached the possibility of using the fur money to board Joel in town so that he could attend school at least part of the year. Cyrus wouldn't hear of it. He spent the money on Christmas instead. Oranges and peppermint candies. A wool cape for her. A skinning knife and a box of lead soldiers for Joel. A doll for Ruth with soft blond hair and eyes that opened and closed and a book of fairy tales.

Allie tried to maintain a schedule of lessons for her son, but he quickly grew bored and restless, picking fights with

Ruth and teasing the little girl until she wailed in misery. Some days when the weather trapped the four of them inside the cabin, Allie had to flee the clamor of their voices and the sunlight raying in off the mirror-bright snow, hiding face down in bed and clamping a pillow around her head.

One night Allie saw the big male wolf for the first time. He stood in the icy moonlight near the sod house. Huge and scrawny. She could feel his hunger reaching out toward the beds where her children slept.

Behind her the springs creaked, and Cyrus said sleepily, "Allie? What're you doin'?"

She went quickly, slipping in beside him to keep him from the window. Pain flowered above her right eye as she endured the heat of his body and his hands kneading her breasts. When he finally slept, Allie crept back to the window. Pinwheels of light fractured her vision, but she saw the yard was empty.

When two calves were stillborn early that spring, Cyrus got it into his head that their bull was defective, and that he would go all the way to Great Falls for another one rather than buy the local stock, which he considered inferior. He admitted then that he had not spent all the fur money after all.

Joel chafed at being left behind, mollified a little by being given the responsibility of the traps. Because the boy was in charge, the traps were laid nearer the house than usual—close enough so they heard the terrible cry echoing in the darkness. Through the night the howling went on and on until Ruth burrowed beside her mother, wailing, hands covering her ears.

The next day Joel was afraid to go into the woods alone, so Allie and Ruth went with him. They found the trap. Empty . . . except for the hideous remains of a leg in the steel jaws, the bone scored by great strong teeth.

Allie was sure the male had been caught in the trap. And now he was out there, maimed and hurt. Dying.

"Damn bastard," Joel cried. "Damn sneaky friggin' bastard."

Allie doubled up a fist and hit the boy so hard he went sprawling. Stunned by the force of the blow and the look in her eyes, he stayed out of her reach and kept his mouth shut while they ranged the woods. Circling vultures eventually led them to the three-legged corpse. Not her night visitor. It was a female, heavy with unborn cubs, her blood staining the pine duff in a great red hemorrhage from the ragged stump where she had chewed her own flesh and bone to escape.

Allie collected the traps and threw them in the sod house, forbidding Joel to touch them. They stayed there until Cyrus came home. She begged him to leave them there, but her pleas didn't move him. The traps went back in the woods.

Allie awoke to the sound of wind again and the rapping of sleet against the window. Her headache was a gleaming blade buried in her temples, but if she moved carefully, she thought she'd be able to bring in a few chunks of oak from the pile outside the door.

She took the rifle along, peering warily into the thick white curtain of falling snow. Nothing. She dragged in the wood and barred the door.

Before the pain worsened, she hacked meat from the deer haunch in the larder, dug out a turnip, a potato; set the food simmering over the fire. While the stew cooked, she found Ruth's book of fairy tales and flipped through the pages until she found the story of Little Red Riding Hood with its black and white drawings.

She stared down at the rough coat, the snarling face, the dripping fangs. The drawing looked nothing like her wolf, nothing at all, and yet it was him. The artist had looked beneath the powerful, savage beauty and drawn the soul of the animal in quick, brutal strokes.

She shivered and moved closer to the fire. And then she heard him—felt him—up on the roof again. Ignoring the smoke. Perhaps drawn by the warmth and the smell of food.

Huddled in the quilts, cold even with the fire blazing, she listened to the wolf shifting in the snow above her. And thought about climbing up beside him and burrowing into his deep, soft fur.

Cyrus caught no more wolves that last summer. He never said so, but Allie knew he somehow blamed her for the empty traps and the sudden bold raids that decimated the calves. He swore there had to be three or four animals left in the pack, but he was wrong. There was only one. She saw the male almost every night, padding into the clearing to stare at the house.

Her headaches came more often and with more ferocity. Some days, alone in the cabin, she would pace the floor and beat her fists against her skull while they raged. Cyrus had always snored. Occasionally he ground his teeth. Now the habit became a nightly occurrence, the noise like a drill boring deep into Allie's skull.

When Cyrus went to town, she sent the children along and stayed at home so that she could have a few blessed hours of silence. Once she thought she would never reconcile herself to the loneliness; now she craved it, and she dreaded more and more the onslaught when her family returned—the children's excited laughter, Cyrus's booming curses and the terrible chewing, grinding, swallowing sounds he made the instant he fell asleep.

She would crouch against the wall, using a pillow to muffle the noise, and ride the scalding waves of torment until sometime in the predawn darkness when the wolf would sing to her, a high pure song of cold stars and dark winter night, and she would finally sleep.

In early November the first snow fell and for days the headaches disappeared. She cleaned the cabin and made gingerbread men and taught Ruth to knit. Cyrus talked of going to town for a few Christmas presents. Not much this year. Money was short, especially after the purchase of the new bull, and there were no wolf pelts to sell. Her fault again. But the snow never stopped, and soon they were shut into the small cabin.

As the days passed, Cyrus battled through the snow to feed the cows and raged at the storm and the wolves. Allie gave up all efforts of teaching the two children their school lessons, so Ruth clicked the knitting needles endlessly, and Joel teased his sister, or else begged his father to teach him to whittle. The sound of their knives was like axes splitting kindling. Joel produced a crude whistle that sent shrill lancets through Allie's skull until she threw it in the fireplace, enduring then his bellows of angry indignation.

And every night the wind picked and rattled and hurled icy pellets at the window while Cyrus made the sounds that might have been a desperate animal chewing at its own flesh and bone.

Days passed.

Weeks.

Pain leaped and roared in Allie's head. Even the wolf song didn't help.

Nothing did until finally, on Christmas Eve she took the Winchester and put an end to the noise.

This time when the snow stopped, the whole world felt muffled in silence. Drifts cocooned the cabin, sealing the door, covering the windows halfway up. The sod house had disappeared, buried in the cold whiteness.

For a time, Allie had heard the cattle bawling, but they had long since died. The cold and the wolf had saved them from slow starvation, and she was glad of that.

She wondered if the wolf was digging down to the corpses. He must be finding food. Otherwise he would leave.

The venison and the vegetables were holding out since she ate so little. She cracked a window to gouge out enough snow to melt for water. The main problem was the cold.

With the weight of the snow blocking the door, she couldn't get to the wood, and she hadn't thought to replenish the reserve inside. She began to burn the furniture. The beds. The table and benches Cyrus had made from heavy yellow pine.

And, finally, her grandmother's walnut chest of drawers.

Ruth's book of fairy tales went for kindling, the pages curling and turning to ash. Allie hesitated over the picture of the ravenous beast that lived in the wolf's heart, crouching close to watch the flames devour the hideous face.

Each night the wolf came to sleep against the warm chimney. She would lie directly below beside the hearth, wrapped in her quilts. And she would listen.

Mostly she would hear the pain that gnawed inside her brain, eating away at the pulpy pink lobes, but sometimes she was sure she heard his massive heart beating, the heavy rhythm lulling her to sleep.

She awoke to the sound of sliding snow and water dripping from the eaves. The door pushed open easily. She brought in wood and built a fire that quickly warmed the cabin.

All that day and the next the sun dazzled so brightly on the snow she stuffed more clothing into the space around the shutters, and retreated under her tent of quilts. The drifts shrank, and that night the wolf couldn't climb up to sleep on the roof.

From the window she could see the dark humps that she knew were the frozen cattle. She thought there would be visitors soon. A trapper. Some kind soul from town to check on them. Oh, they would come, and, when they did, they would find what lay in the sod house. Only a matter of time.

She stripped the last meat from the haunch of venison, then finally boiled the heavy thighbone with the remaining shriveled vegetables. The wolf appeared each night to wait with her. And every day the weather grew steadily warmer. One morning when she went outside for wood, she could smell the decaying cattle in the yard and the same foul odor coming from the sod house.

That night she let the fire die, stirred the ashes and beat out the last sparks. Then she paced the dark cabin, each step cleaving her skull and stoking the terrible fire that burned in her head.

A cleansing—the doctor had been right at last—because the pain consumed the last of her fear and left only icy calm.

The moon rose, flooding the world with chill white light, and when she saw the wolf lope into the clearing, she opened the door, pulling it fully open, and lay down on the pile of quilts in the barren room.

And when he came to her in the cold stillness, she plunged her hands up into his rough fur to touch his warmth and feel the hammer stroke of his heart before she lifted her throat to the sharp teeth and the final, blessed silence.

Is You Is or Is You Ain't Miranda?

Miranda dreamed again.

Always the same dream. Trapped in a lightless, soundless void, a nothingness so vast it isolated the soul.

"Are you falling?" her shrink had asked—one of them, she didn't remember which one.

"You mean like in the dreams I had when I was a kid?" Scary dreams, the ground rushing up to offer its hard embrace. *"No, just—caught."*

She started to explain she would welcome the sensation of falling—how motion would anchor her in that great empty vacuum—until she caught the look in his eyes.

She awoke with a start, suppressing a throat-wracking scream to a whimper. Disoriented, and so cold, her flesh chilled as marble. The clock beside the bed read 12:01, greenish numbers glowing in the dark room. Beside her, Brian rolled over, turning his back, making a point with a crack of bedsprings. Even asleep he sensed she was having another one of her strange experiences, and he resented it. A solid, practical man, Brian had long since lost patience with her inability to buck up, keep her chin high, to soldier on against this affliction he saw as a failure of character.

She got out of bed, careful not to touch his warm body. In the hall closet was a heavy flannel robe, fleece-lined slippers. Miranda put them on, hugged the robe tightly around her, and went quietly—warily—downstairs.

"What exactly do you see that's different?" her shrink had asked.

135

"Most of the time things are just—wrong."

This was before she discovered she couldn't trust these curious, sympathetic doctors who nodded their understanding without believing a word she said.

"It's subtle. I don't even notice at first. Sometimes—the worse times—it's as though I've stumbled into a room lined with funhouse mirrors."

Tonight the walls were flat, the stair rail smooth beneath her hand. In the kitchen the gas flame burned blue beneath the white porcelain of the teakettle. She sipped steaming Constant Comment standing in front of the sink and watched a bone-white moon spill light over the back yard, so bright the shrubs and trees left inky shadows on the lawn.

Everything was familiar and right, but the sense of wrongness was there, bringing along its freight of dread.

"Just relax, Mrs. Croft, and lie very still," the neurologist had said before they put her in the confined cylinder for the scans that would look for lesions or other abnormalities.

She had fought her terror in the metal coffin and let them look, hoping there would be something that could be excised, something real that could be probed, bombarded, cut away—knowing all along the tests would be normal.

Tea finished and cup rinsed, she went back to the living room. The upstairs hovered, mocking her with unexplored darkness. She couldn't go up there. The light would wake up Brian. Instead she explored the downstairs, scrutinizing every inch of beige carpet and striped wallpaper. She smelled furniture polish mixed with the faint odor of last night's roasted lamb, listened to the mechanical pulse of appliances, ran her fingers over the cherry wood tables as though the strangeness would be embossed on the grain like a message in Braille.

She found nothing wrong. Nothing.

Finally, exhausted but warmed at last by her frantic exploration, she curled up on the couch and slept.

The sound of the shower awakened her so that she could hurry out to the kitchen to start coffee and make toast for Brian. She could feel her lips stretched over her teeth as she smiled and pretended things were normal.

Maybe pretending helped make it so because by the time Brian left for work and she was ready to go out, the sunlight was turning the tulips to scarlet satin, and in the market the carrots looked just the right shade of orange, the lettuces displayed in a suitable palette of greens.

That night, for a week of nights, Miranda went to bed and didn't dream at all; she even made love to Brian, and got up to a perfectly normal world.

Myranda started awake from that cold, dark void, a scream caught in her throat, her skin like ice. She got up, careful not to awaken Bryan, wrapped herself in a warm robe, and went quietly—warily—downstairs.

Everything was familiar and right. The doctors were right. This feeling of wrongness was all in her head.

While the purple gas flame hissed under the teakettle, she opened the refrigerator to comfort herself with its contents: a bag of red carrots, a sheaf of yellow lettuce. Then she stood at the sink to drink her tea and watched the wash of faint light give way to a bright white glow as the second moon rose in the west . . .

"Ha' chick noo," Carol said, her voice like a rusty old gate creaking open.

Mark, feeding her, stared, his mouth rounding in shock, the spoon tipping over and spilling the food, splattering both his grimy clothes and hers.

"What did you say?"

"Chic-ken noo—dle," she repeated. "I hate it." Her eyes, always vague and disconnected, now focused and she said, "Mark? My God, what have you done to your hair?"

He dropped the spoon and his trembling hand went to the thinning gray strands, which he cut haphazardly to keep out of his eyes, realizing how he must look to her, thinking it was a good thing that she couldn't see herself.

Her skin was smooth, there was that at least, but it was pasty white the same as his, and her hair was even grayer. She wasn't fat—how could she be?—but her body looked as though the musculature had settled into lumps around her bones.

"I'm a wreck," he said shakily. "Sure, I know it. Don't worry. Doesn't matter. Makes no difference at all, because we're all right, baby, do you understand? All *right,* and I'll explain it to you, I'll tell you—"

"Mark, what is this place?" She was staring past him at the cavern looming overhead. "It's a game, right? Some kind of stupid party you've dragged me to."

"No, honey, no, it's—"

He looked around, wishing the place looked better. He

had tried once to decorate the dark walls, witness the ancient loops of shredding tinsel, the remnants of bed sheets printed with huge cabbage roses, a string of green and white plastic pennants that spelled out *Earl's Used Cars.* He'd even splattered on gallons of Sunshine Yellow paint. No matter, in the dim lighting driven off an outside solar panel the place still looked like the cave nature had carved from sullen, gray stone.

"Now I remember," she said. "You *asshole.* You gave me something, didn't you? You brought me here even after I told you it was crazy, that I didn't want to leave Chicago—"

She broke off, her eyes fixed beyond him and huge with shock. He followed her gaze over to the cave entrance.

He was used to the kids, of course, but he saw Missy now as Carol must see her: a spindly, rat-faced, naked little creature with skin the color of dirty putty and eyes all huge black pupils with just a rim of silvery iris.

He caught his wife as she toppled over, laid her down gently, then crouched beside her to watch the shallow rising and falling of her chest.

The child stood where she was, silent and incurious, holding the bat skeleton she always carried around. He'd found her Ninja Turtles and even a Barbie doll, but she preferred the bones that lay in piles in the outer caves, the flesh long desiccated and fallen away. Liked to rub them against a fungus that had started to grow on the cave walls and glow a phosphorescent green—and he didn't want to think what *that* meant.

Right now he needed to concentrate on Carol. She had just fainted this time, he was pretty sure that's all that had happened. So he had to get ready for when she woke up again.

He said to the little girl, "Missy, honey, go get your brother and sister. We all need to talk about Mom."

He was ashamed to admit it, but Carol had been right about one thing: He had indeed given her something all those years ago, 45 milligrams of Dalmane to be exact—part of the stash of assorted drugs he'd accumulated from the Osco Drug store he managed. Otherwise, he'd never have gotten her into the van for the drive to Kentucky.

And a damn good thing he had, too. Away from the cities, the denial was not so complete. There had been a few blockades, random gangs that he narrowly escaped, a nightmare journey that Carol had been spared. And once back in the hills where he spent his childhood, it had not been an easy thing to find the caves, even though he had a vivid memory of his father taking him there when he was seven and the old man had talked about that day incessantly before he died, reeled back in time by the grim barbs of his senility.

While Mark blundered through a tangle of blackberry brambles, Carol was in the van, serenely drugged and snuggled into a nest of blankets. She only came out of the stupor for a brief moment once they were safely inside the caves. One look, then her eyes went huge and fixed and she became the walking zombie she had been for the past fourteen years. Mark had no idea what the medical term was for her state, but once he'd seen a kid at camp sleepwalking and that was the closest thing he could think to compare to Carol's condition.

She would open her mouth and let him spoon in food and obediently take care of other bodily functions. While she didn't respond to sex, she never pushed him away, and God knows he'd needed whatever contact and comfort he could get, although sometimes the idea flashed through his mind that he was doing it with a corpse. When the babies were born, her response to the delivery was a dazed, dumb pain that reminded him of those cows and dogs forever giving birth on the old public TV shows.

The kids—well, they'd looked a little funny, but he'd been so happy to have them, little scraps of himself and Carol. Parents can love anything, can't they? They are supposed to, for God's sake.

The three sidled in now. Tim and Amy were like tall gray shadows, not wearing a stitch of clothes just like their little sister, remarkably alike except for the genitals.

Beside him Carol moaned and suddenly Mark knew this was a mistake. It was no good to have Carol see them too soon, suffer another shock, maybe return to that sleepwalking state.

Even as he thought this, the kids backed out into the narrow hall that led to another room in the maze of caves. He followed and tried to explain the situation.

"See, this is a big surprise to your mom," he said. "All this time I thought—on some level—but, well, I guess she never knew what was happening. So we need to take this a step at a time. Okay, guys? I know you're disappointed, but if you could just give me some time alone with her—"

He heard a clattering back in the main chamber and knew that Carol must be awake. The children didn't have to be told; they glided away without a backward glance, leaving him feeling much more relieved than he should have been as he hurried to their mother.

She was down on her knees, going through a pile of things he had heaped in a corner, miscellaneous junk he'd collected just in case he found a use for it. As he rushed over, she seized an old rearview mirror from the pile and stared into it, her face loose with horror.

"Oh my God," she wailed. "Oh my God!"

When he grabbed her shoulders, she beat at him with the mirror, slicing his skin on a sharp burr of chrome, both of them streaked with his blood by the time her rage was finally spent and she collapsed in his arms to weep for the world that she understood now was lost forever.

After all those ticking doomsday clocks, after the brush fire wars and waves of global terrorism, the world had not ended with a thermonuclear bang. It had just stopped dead in something frightened scientists referred to as gores—pieces of the world's sphere in grapefruit-like sections, pole to pole, about 138 miles wide at the equator. This kill zone was almost precisely two degrees, which at first everybody thought had to be significant, but in the end only meant it would take 180 incidents to finish off civilization.

Incidents—that was one word frequently used to describe what was happening. Phenomenon was another. Nobody knew what to call that ominous pulse of energy that lit up the hemisphere north to south. CNN and the networks all had twenty-four hour coverage after the first incident that took out a section down through Great Bear Lake in the Northwest Territories in Canada, Grand Prairie in Alberta, Spokane, Reno, and Los Angeles. Like everybody else, Mark was at home watching all those field reporters looking grim and scared, waiting for the little robots that looked like square tank-type vacuum cleaners to come out of the kill zone and give everybody a clue as to what the hell had happened. If indeed they imparted some information, the scientists obviously had no idea how to decode it.

There were theories galore. Laser beams generated in the heart of the universe. Another civilization sterilizing the earth before colonization. A second swath through Moscow, Jiddah, Nairobi, and Prince Edward Island had nipped in the bud the immediate suspicion that the Soviets were up to their old tricks.

By the fifth incident it became apparent that the earth was

like a chicken on a spit and the strikes were some kind of energy pulse of unknown origin and entirely random. And it was obvious that despite their robots and computers, science was not going to pull a miraculous rabbit out of its technological hat. At that point the shock had worn off and the view through the robotic cameras had a strangely calming effect, all those eerily silent streets strewn with corpses that did not decay because even the bacteria were dead. Most of mankind simply pulled into its shell, turtle-like, and entered into a pact of ultimate denial.

The non-stop TV coverage, the panels of stammering scientists and terrified politicians, and the fundamentalists who ranted about the approaching Rapture gave way to snowy static as stations stopped transmitting or to old reruns, every show with a laugh track.

Voices of doom on the Internet shrieked until enough strands of the worldwide web broke and the system collapsed. With electricity rationed, the system was moot anyway. It was during one of the last times Mark sneaked a half-hour online that he caught a desperate message: "We have to hide ourselves. Find the deepest hole and crawl into it. Couldn't that work? Couldn't it?"

The power went off then. Mark never knew who sent that message, where the person lived, if he or she had survived to find a hiding place. But the desperate question had jogged Mark's memory and jarred him from his apathy, set him planning and scheming to at least try for survival.

He accumulated gas for the van; bedrolls and warm clothing; supplies of food, medicine, candles, and batteries. Just enough for Carol and him. He had no close family left. She came from a huge clan that all lived within ten blocks of each other, a squabbling, contentious bunch that couldn't agree on where to bury their mother until the undertaker threatened to charge them rent on the body. Taking any of them along was never a consideration.

So much planning, so many obstacles. Then they were in the caves, and he thought for a while he had not found a haven after all, that he had descended into hell instead.

He held Carol now and tried to explain it all to her. The suffocating blackness of that deep, inner cavern where he had taken her and where they stayed for almost a year, allowing himself only a few hours a day of precious light from candles and a battery-powered lantern. How a week after their arrival, he'd awakened to find the rock around them lit by a pale white luminance, the mountain itself pierced by a light so brilliant that the stone was rendered transparent. He could have looked right out into the heart of the beast, if he'd had the nerve to keep his eyes open.

He told her about the hunger that finally forced him out; about that first awful foray into the nearest town. Later the bodies would become mummified, but then they just seemed frozen like in one of those movies about time travel. People, animals, birds—dead in flight and fallen from the sky. Without bacteria to start the process of decay, even the steaks in the supermarket meat case hadn't spoiled, although they had begun to dry out. He had grabbed up a vanload of supplies and fled in terror back to the caves, sure that there was some residual contamination that would kill him and leave Carol to starve.

He told her how the terror gradually dimmed, how he'd brought them here to this cavern nearer the entrance where there was some light. And he told her about the birth of the children.

"They're—different—I guess, and no wonder, everything that's happened. But they're such good kids, Carol. They mind so well, never give me a minute's trouble. You'll get use to them. You will. Carol . . ."

He trailed off in despair. Neither his arms nor his words had anchored Carol and kept her from slipping away, back into her sleepwalking fugue.

He sat and held her, vaguely aware of time passing, of the three children hovering in the entrance. He knew he should talk to them, but the grief was a private knife in his heart, keeping him mute. To have Carol come back and then lose her again—all he could do was sit there and ask himself how he could go on without her.

The answer came like a whispered thought. He didn't have to go on. He could end it all right now. A quiet painless death for them both, he still had a plentiful supply of drugs. He'd thought about death often enough over the years, just couldn't bring himself to commit the necessary acts. Himself and Carol, maybe, but not the children, and he couldn't abandon them, young and dependent as they were. But now the older kids were self-sufficient, and they would take care of Missy . . .

Once started, the death thoughts were like a flood tide building, sweeping away his trepidation and stilling a voice back in his head that was crying, "Wait . . ."

Are they gone now?
Soon.
He was kinda nice. You're sure you had to—
*It was time, Missy/*They'll be happier.
I guess.
And it's better for us now./*Not so noisy.*/We don't have to talk out loud.
Yesss, but I still can't hear the others.
You will.

145

Are there lots more of us?

Not lots./Enough.

Will they ever come here so we can see them?

Maybe. Someday./*Come on. It's over. Time to take them out-*
side.

The big light won't be on will it?

Of course not.

Good. I just like the little lights and the one with a face.
Can we stay outside a while? Can we go see the town place? I
wanna move the bones and play "What the Old Ones Did."

Sure, Missy, we can do that./We can do anything we want.

Black Is the Color of My True Love's Heart

The heart is the central organ of the blood-vascular system and consists of a hollow muscle, placed between the lungs and enclosed in the cavity of the pericardium . . .

Robert lies and stares at me, his eyes dull and vacant in a face that has become a cave of bone. With his immunity gone the list of infections that assault my brother is long and ghastly. This current battle is with *Pneumocystis carinii*, and the microbes are winning, making every breath a struggle.

The heart, in the adult, measures five inches in length, three inches and a half in breadth in the broadest part, and two inches and a half in thickness.

I think my brother no longer understands the words, but that he takes comfort from the sound of my voice, so I read for hours every day: *A Tale of Two Cities*, *I, Robot*, most of *The International Thesaurus of Quotations*, and now *Gray's Anatomy*.

The heart's prevalent weight, in the male, varies from ten to twelve ounces; in the female, from eight to ten . . .

I ought to find some comfort here myself. At least I know it's impossible for the fist-size lump of muscle in my chest to break as I sit vigil for this final disintegration of my family.

I discovered Robert's copy of *Gray's Anatomy* along with his medical bag and a stack of his other books back in the big storage closet in the basement of my house, deposited there when he tested HIV positive and made the decision to leave his internship at Cook County Hospital. More of his things were added a year ago when he went into the hospice.

This was originally our parents' house, the place where we grew up—Robert, Megan, and me. Big and solid, the building had a look of being as firmly rooted as the half-dozen huge old maples on the half-acre lot. The basement closet had been a favorite hideout on cold winter days like these for games of hide and seek. Now, it has become a repository of painful memories and broken dreams.

"I only have myself to blame," Robert told me one night while he was still coherent, then later when his fever spiked, he seized my hand and whispered, "You can still leave him, Janie, you can . . ."

But that was months ago and, of course, I dismissed what he said, reminding myself of things I'd read about AIDS, how the diseases that flourish in its wake affect the mind.

Behind Robert's belongings there are two boxes crammed with the parts of my younger sister Megan's life that none of us could bear to throw away. One contains pieces of her childhood—among them a ratty baby blanket, Mom's hand-made version of the *Goodnight, Moon* bunny with one eye missing and a seam leaking stuffing, a pink tutu that shy Megan wore for her one painfully awkward ballet recital but would never part with. In the other carton are the blue-lined composition books she filled with her poetry and two copies of the literary magazine that printed her only published work.

Yesterday I brought a box of my own to add to the collection. Crouched there in the musty darkness, I listened to the throb of the furnace and remembered, suddenly, a day of sunlight and clear skies when Megan and I lay on spring-green grass and looked up at the canopy of maple limbs arching above us, intertwined, bursting with new leaves. Megan was three and I was eight.

"Look, Janie," Megan had said. "The trees are holding hands. They're keeping out the storm clouds."

I was old enough to know the maples couldn't hold the violent April storms at bay, young enough to feel protected, nonetheless. There were plenty of bad things in the world, out there somewhere beyond our lot line. The scary images came in nightly TV newscasts, in stern lectures at school about Mr. Stranger Danger. But we were safe, guarded by our red brick house and sentinel trees and a close, loving family.

Back then who could have imagined that our trust in love was the thing that would destroy us all?

The heart consists of four chambers or cavities, two forming the right half, the right auricle and right ventricle, and two the left half, the left auricle and left ventricle. The right half of the heart contains venous or impure blood; the left, arterial or pure blood . . .

I break off reading when the phone rings on the table beside Robert's bed. Nobody else ever calls so I know it's Peter and that it must be four o'clock. During the ten years we've been married, Peter has phoned from work at the same time every weekday when he was not away on business. Until I began going to the hospice and then coming here to the hospital when Robert's condition deteriorated, I was always at home, waiting to fly to the phone and plan our evenings. I wonder now why it took me so long to add up the number of times these calls meant I would be canceling reservations or scraping most of the meal I was cooking into the disposal since my husband never eats leftovers.

"Jane? Just checking in," he says and I'm amazed at how, even now, his rich, deep voice can make me slightly breathless.

I can picture him at his desk, managing to look both thoughtlessly casual and coolly elegant. The thick, dark hair is barbered every week. His suits come fresh from a cleaner's bag every morning.

I may have let a few pounds accumulate, care little whether I'm wearing old gray sweats or tattered jeans, and never think these days of regular visits to the beauty salon for coloring to hide the gray prematurely streaking my auburn hair. Peter would never allow distraction or grief to alter the routines that keep his body and wardrobe as perfectly maintained as they were on our wedding day.

"He's slipping away," I tell him, although Peter hasn't asked about Robert; he never asks.

"Well, what do you expect?" He makes no attempt to hide the callousness in his voice. "Listen, stay there as long as you like. Something's come up here so I'll be late."

"Fine," I say. "Whatever."

When I hang up and turn back to Robert, his eyes are fastened on me, alive with mute longing. I can feel the numbness that has gripped me these past few days giving way to a quick burst of scalding rage. Just the knowledge that Peter was on the other end of that phone was enough to drag my brother back for an agonizing moment. Worst of all, before Robert slips away again, I see that for him love has never mutated into the liberating fire of hate.

Blood is an opaque, rather viscid fluid, of a bright-red or scarlet color when it flows from the arteries, of a dark- red or purple color when it flows from the veins . . .

I keep reading until my voice grows hoarse and I am whispering the words.

The left auriculo-ventricular opening is behind the sternum . . . The right auriculo-ventricular opening is a little lower . . . as a sufficient practical guide for the definition of the portion of the heart which is uncovered by lung or pleura: Make a circle of two inches in diameter round a point midway between the nipple and the end of the sternum . . .

I break off and sit for a minute, staring at the window on the other side of Robert's bed. Outside, the November darkness has arrived early and a fine sleet beats at the glass. My brother's eyes are closed, his breathing shallow and labored. His gaunt face is the color of old, gray putty. I ring for the nurse, but I don't need nurses or doctors to tell me that he has slipped back into a coma and the end is very near.

It's eight thirty when I get to Cedar Hill Sanatorium. The staff is not happy to have their routines interrupted, but, under the circumstances, grudgingly allow me to see my mother. I wait in a small room with French doors that open onto a patio. A pleasant enough place in summer, but now there's nothing to see outside but black night and cold rain.

A burly middle-aged attendant in a blue jumpsuit brings Mom to me. When they come in, I can hear a burst of laugh track from the TV down the hall and a rhythmic pounding that I don't want to speculate about.

Mom clings to the man's arm, looking frail and disconnected. All three of her children towered over her, but until now I've never really realized how tiny she is. Two weeks ago I agreed to let them cut her hair to try and keep her from pulling it out. It's about half an inch long, the stark style revealing the shape of her beautiful skull—and the ugly patches of torn scalp.

"Janie?" she says uncertainly and clutches a robe closed over her nightgown.

"She just got her meds, Miz Keirson." The attendant sounds defensive and shifts his weight as though his feet hurt. "We just started gettin' everybody ready for bed."

I've done battle with Peter over the cost of this private clinic. I've kept close tabs and called the staff on anything I judged less than adequate care, but tonight I don't have the strength for even a minor confrontation.

"Give us fifteen minutes," I say, and when he leaves, I put my arm around my mother and guide her over to a small sofa. She smells of baby powder and sweat. Up close I can see a spot the size of a pencil eraser, red and raw, above her right ear.

"We were watching Dick van Dyke," Mom says. "Your dad always hated sit-coms, do you remember that?"

"Yes, Mom, I remember."

"History, airplanes, stuff about the wars, that's all he liked."

She begins to probe at the raw spot on her head and I grab her wrist. She slipped into depression after Megan died, but it was Daddy's fatal stroke that sent her here. Selling the business, that was the mistake, but the offer was substantial, both of them had lost the heart to go on, and Peter had convinced us that it was the right thing to do. Within two years the company was sucked dry and discarded while my father watched helplessly. I think he simply couldn't bear seeing something he put his life into destroyed.

"Where's Robbie?" Mom asks in a querulous tone. "When is he coming to see me?"

"I'm sorry, Mom. Robbie—"

"You're the only one I trust to do this," Robert said when he gave me his durable power of attorney for health care. So there were no machines, no attempt at resuscitation, and only me to hear him draw his last breath.

"He has AIDS, you know," Mom whispers with a fearful look toward the door. "Don't tell anybody here. They might not let him in."

"I won't tell," I promise, and then I just hold her and listen to her vague ramblings until the attendant returns.

I sit on the floor of the basement closet with the contents

of the boxes a jumble around me: Robert's medical bag, Megan's composition books, toys we could never bear to part with, trophies—and pictures, so many pictures. Here are all the moments frozen in time, a record of the happy memories of a happy family.

They say that photographs don't lie. I know it's true as I turn the pages of my wedding album. I was not the only one in love with Peter Keirson. We all were.

He was the handsome, thoughtful husband my mother wanted for her daughter, the bright, ambitious surrogate son who was more than happy to help my father run the business and allow Robert to finish medical school without feeling guilty. On one page I glimpse Robert's desperate attraction and Megan's dazzled yearning. And I remember how Peter coaxed her out on the dance floor, how I loved him for giving my shy, awkward sister a few minutes of graceful beauty as she floated in his arms.

I notice now that Megan avoided the camera after that night. I think she must have seen what these pictures revealed, even if none of the rest of us did. There is one photo of her at the party my parents gave Peter and me on our first anniversary. It's a group shot, the happy family whole for the last time, everybody touching each other except for Megan, who stands stiffly apart.

Shortly after my wedding she ignored my parents' hurt misgivings and moved into a small, shabby apartment on Chicago's near north side. The place had heavy old windows. The warped wooden frames efficiently sealed in the gas when, four weeks after our anniversary party, she turned off the pilot light and opened all the burners on the stove.

"Jane?" Peter calls from the top of the basement stairs. I don't answer, but he comes anyway and stands in the closet doorway, looking down at me. His hair, damp with rain, has a wet gleam.

He says, "I knew you'd be in here."

In the past I guess he had the decency or the craftiness to shower before he came home. Not tonight. He not only smells of liquor, he reeks of a musky perfume and has that lazy, sated look I recognize.

"You ought to get rid of this stuff," he says. "It's becoming an obsession, pouring over this junk."

"He's dead, Peter." The words are a knife in my throat. "Megan—Dad, now Robert. And Mom—I couldn't tell her."

"I'm sorry, Janie, but at least he's not suffering anymore." The words may have the right ring to them, but the pity in his eyes contains not one spark of tenderness or empathy.

He takes a step toward me and reaches out a hand, but I shrink away. He stares at me and says softly, "You really better watch it, Jane, or you're going to wind up in that nuthouse with your mother." He leaves then, saying, "Stay in here all night if you want, I'm going to bed."

I sit there and remember how soon after we were married that I realized Peter would never be a faithful husband and how quickly I learned to live with the knowledge. As some judge once said, "Cats roam because it's their nature." It's what I told myself and how I coped, but maybe the misery of the knowing was an acid, eating away. Maybe I am going crazy and the things that have happened are just the work of a cold, uncaring fate and nothing to do with Peter.

I draw a shaky breath and pick up one of Megan's composition books. The only thing of hers I've read is her published poem. I knew the way she felt about her work, that it was intensely personal. My God, it so horrified me to think that strangers would read them—that when Robert called from her apartment to tell me what he'd found, even choking with despair, I said, "Her work, Robbie, don't let anybody—"

"Of course," he said, "yes. I'll take care of it."

And he had, putting the books in a box and taking them out of the apartment before he called the police.

It occurs to me now that Megan's suicide might not have been a rash act, that she had time to destroy her poems before she killed herself. That maybe she left them for a reason.

The books are dated, down in the corner: a month, day, and year. I have seen her write these dates and know it marked the time she began each book. I find the one dated just after my wedding, the next to the last one, and open it. By the time I finish and read a few pages of the final one, I know.

Seduction, followed by disinterest, I've learned my husband's pattern well. Learned to live with it, but Megan couldn't. And if I'm right about Peter and Megan, then all the rest follows.

My dad's company—the big wave of corporate raiding was about over, but there were still sharks circling, cruising for stable, cash-heavy morsels, and Peter churned the waters. The oddest thing was that later when he was offered a new corporate job in acquisitions, none of us felt any outrage because of this. He was so penitent over the way he'd misjudged the situation, so torn over whether to accept the position. Besides, Mom and Dad and I had grimmer worries.

Even though Robert was devastated by Megan's suicide, he managed to stay focused on his studies until he got his M.D. I remember our quiet celebration, the medical bag that was my parents' gift with "all the tools of the trade," my dad said, his pride tempered by lingering grief.

I remember something else, too: all the time Peter spent with Robert that summer, the little worm of suspicion that so sickened me I quickly banished the thoughts.

There would be nothing of Robert's to tell me if what I suspected then, suspected now, was true. It didn't matter.

Whatever happened between the two of them, the results were the same. Robert began to deliberately withdraw from us. There was a reckless shine in his eyes and an evasive tone in his voice that terrified me. This went on into the fall, when he began his internship. The work seemed to recenter him, and I began to think I'd been wrong. That he was a doctor after all. He, of all people, knew the consequences of risky behavior.

"I only have myself to blame," Robert had said, and then, "You can leave him, Janie, you can . . ."

But it is far too late for that.

The heart measures five inches in length, three inches and a half in breadth . . .

I go up the two flights of stairs from the basement to our bedroom. Peter has left on the lamp that sits on a table by the window. A three-way bulb is turned to its lowest wattage but gives plenty of light to show Peter sprawled on his back and sleeping soundly. Crisp, dark hair defines the muscles of his naked chest and descends in a V to the sheet drawn up around his waist. I can see him breathing in and out, the bones of his rib cage.

Make a circle of two inches in diameter round a midway point between the nipple and the end of the sternum . . .

Wind hurls icy pellets against the window. The scalpel I took from Robert's medical bag feels just as cold in my hand. Some resistance, like cutting through elastic, then the knife goes in easily between the ribs, startling Peter awake so he gets to see my face as the blade plunges deep and sure.

The heart is an efficient pump. Scarlet arterial blood and purple venal blood mix and seep down the side of the bed and onto the floor, quickly staining the brown carpet a true, deep shade of black.